I found my assailant trying to climb up the sheer wall of the canyon. Without climbing equipment, the attempt had to end in failure. Not even a spider could make it up the sheer face without a lot of help from somewhere. I stood, rifle cradled gently, in the crook of my left arm.

Slipping, almost falling, my assailant glared at me.

"Bastard!" she sneered.

"You aren't as good as you thought, Elaine. Your makeup is smudged," I said softly.

"Go to hell!" screamed Elaine.

I raised the laser, aimed and fired . . .

FROM THE NICK CARTER
KILLMASTER SERIES

A Killmaster Spy Chiller

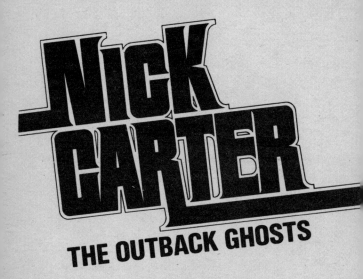

NICK CARTER

THE OUTBACK GHOSTS

CHARTER BOOKS, NEW YORK

THE OUTBACK GHOSTS

A Charter Book/published by arrangement with
The Condé Nast Publications, Inc.

Charter edition/March 1983

ISBN: 0-441-64433-3

Charter Books are published by Charter Communications, Inc.
200 Madison Avenue, New York, New York 10016.
PRINTED IN THE UNITED STATES OF AMERICA

Dedicated to the men of the
Secret Services of the
United States of America

ONE

I hefted the unwieldly M-16, studying the laser attachment at the muzzle end of the barrel. What the black box lacked in maneuverability it more than made up for in accuracy. The laser beam never missed; it sped instantaneously directly to the spot aimed.

For me, Nick Carter, Killmaster for AXE, that was important.

I hunkered down on the windward side of a large sand dune. The breeze kicking up due to thermal differentials on the barren land nearly froze me. Sunrise was less than an hour away and by the time the sun peaked over the craggy mountains to the west, I intended to be finished with my mission.

If everything went okay. If this bulky laser rifle didn't misfire. If the convoy was on schedule. And most important, if the person stalking me didn't get me into a set of sights before I eliminated the men guarding the convoy.

I'd tried every trick in the book to throw off my tracker. They'd all failed. The person following me was good, damned good. If I took my finger off the numbers for even an instant, a tiny beam of light might seek out my body, ending my mission then and there. Such thoughts only slowed me down, created tiny self-doubts. I checked my Rolex. Forty-six minutes till dawn. Time remained for me to try one more tactic to flush out my pursuer. I was confident of success with my ambush on the daily supply convoy. Removing the hunter so doggedly snapping at my heels would insure success.

1

The winter-time desert tried to claim my fingers and toes with frostbite. My nose dripped and, as a result, I barely smelled the sharp scent of creosote bush. I refused to give in. My body had to obey me and not the dictates of externals like cold and wind and allergy-producing bushes that hardly grew higher than my head. Moving along the ridge of hulking sand dunes, I came to a Joshua tree. The tortured arms reached out in an eerie, questing embrace. I knew better than to get too close. The rough, spiny surface would rip away at my flesh. The last thing in the world I needed was another set of cuts and the eventual scars. I'd had enough of both.

Peering over the rim, I caught a blast of sand full in the face. Spitting out the fine grit along with precious moisture, I squinted and tried to spot any shape moving in the bare, bleak desert behind me. Nothing. I hadn't expected it. I knew my adversary too well. Not a single mistake had been made so far on either of our parts, and I doubted either of us would start now. We were both professionals; we killed for a living.

I slipped over the rim and crawled on my belly down the far side of the dune. When I came to a rocky arroyo, I got my feet under me and began a dogtrot to the west. My assignment position lay east, on a small mesa overlooking the highway. My shadow wouldn't know that. With a little luck, my scheme would lure the hunter off course.

"Good," I said, smiling to myself when I heard a faint, distant click of rock tumbling into the arroyo. The temptation mounted to turn and try to ambush my pursuer. That wouldn't do. I might be taken out. The mission came first. Always.

I stepped up my pace until I almost ran. In the dimness of starlight this amounted to suicide. Slip once, sprain an ankle. Slip twice, break a leg. And that meant a ruby lance of laser would knife into my chest. Instinctively, I touched a small circular medallion on my jacket. Another rested on my back and a half dozen others were spotted around my clothing. I considered rubbing dirt onto them or even pulling them off, then decided against this. I wanted to keep the contest fair.

I wanted to prove who was the best.

Scouting the area before sunset had given me a good idea of the lay. The arroyo twisted and turned downward until it came to the edge of the mesa. From a point about fifty yards from the precipice, the arroyo sloped more steeply to tumble off the side of the mountain. In spring a veritable waterfall would occur, changing this dry stream bed into a raging torrent, both here and far below on the desert floor.

As I kicked out the stick bracing a pile of rocks I'd prepared earlier, a few loose stones began rattling down the incline. The larger rocks followed and finally a boulder began a slow, crushing tumble to eventually fall over the mesa edge.

The clamor continued for long minutes. I hoped it would make my pursuer pause, then consider all the possibilities. If it did nothing more, I'd be long gone on my way to the completion of my mission. If the shadowy figure came to investigate, I might get really lucky. The loose gravel in the arroyo might yield and send an unwilling body over the edge.

Knowing my adversary as I did, the best I could hope for was buying a little time with confusion.

A quick glance at my watch showed twenty-four minutes till sunrise. I picked up the pace, running on the alternately sandy and rocky terrain. The cold air knifed into my lungs and sent renewed energy surging in my veins. The desert began to come alive around me—the timid life poking up from burrows in search of food; the predators waiting for their prey to forage.

I felt at home here. I was a predator.

With less than five minutes to go, I flopped onto my belly, the cumbersome laser rifle thrust in front of me. I settled down, got tiny pockets dug in the sand to cradle my elbows and the barrel of the rifle, then waited, taking long, deep breaths to recover from my run. When the moment of truth came, I wanted to be rock-steady.

Leave it to the bureaucrats to never be a second late, I thought as the supply convoy lumbered out of a mountain gap and started down the narrow asphalt road. My shot would be at a distance of about three hundred yards. Quite a ways with a slug-throwing rifle. A snap with a laser.

A tiny breeze whipped up, then settled down. Sunrise on the desert is normally calm, dead calm. I intended to make it a little deader.

The convoy rounded the last curve and stretched out in front of me. I sighted on the driver in the lead truck, then hesitated. This had to be played out according to the book all the way, no violations of my orders, no matter how trivial. I reached up and pulled down a pair of protective goggles. The landscape darkened appreciably and made the shot more difficult. It didn't matter. My finger curled back and performed a perfect squeeze.

I expected recoil. None came. The box fastened to the barrel hummed slightly. Nothing more. But my shot had found its target. The leading truck swerved and went off the road. I aimed, fired and aimed again as quickly as I could. The soldiers boiled out of the trucks, looking around like so many army ants for the termite daring to invade their hill. They never found me. My laser found them instead.

By the time they realized how deadly accurate my aim was, it was all over for them. The trucks were destroyed. A dozen drivers and soldiers were out of action. That convoy would never reach its intended target on time—or ever.

I stopped firing and let the black box cool down. Heat boiled backward from it to warm my left hand on the rifle stock. The instant the electronic humming died down I heard a slight crunch of a heavy boot touching dried sand, going through the crusty sun-baked surface. The step was light; the person behind the step weighed only a hundred and five pounds.

Jerking hard and fast to one side, I rolled and kicked up sand to obscure my assailant's vision. A slight hiss told how close the enemy laser beam came to my head. I felt a moment's rage. It wasn't supposed to be like this. That beam was intended to be absolutely silent, absolutely fast. I might have been killed.

I had slipped from my cool, efficient Killmaster mode when it became obvious the convoy had been stopped and my mission successful. I'd done then what no agent should ever do: gloat over victory. This instant of carelessness had almost been my undoing.

The laser rifle pulled around, and I returned fire. The goggles hindered me, but I left them in position. There wasn't time to push them back. Another beam of ruby light zinged by my head. I doubted my attacker had protective goggles on. A safety violation, of course, but winning counted more.

"I got 'em already," I shouted, dropping behind a lava rock the size of a Toyota truck. "Give it up. There's no reason to keep after me. I've won."

"Sure," came the soft voice. "You've won. But I can win, too, by taking you out. Come on, Nick, be a good boy. Let me get in one good shot so I can score a few points."

"Well," I said, as if actually thinking about such a ridiculous proposal. It didn't fool either of us. We're pros. I moved fast and quiet, working my way to the edge of the mesa. With a little luck, I might find a canyon leading down to the desert floor. The more distance—and solid rock—between me and the laser rifle in my assailant's hands, the better I liked it.

Staying alert saved me. If I'd stayed put a laser beam would have found me for sure. As it was, a dim silhouette formed against the first gray light of dawn. I dropped, aimed and fired in one smooth motion. The laser beam shot true; my aim was off. The target moved away even as I fired.

"Nick, I'm ashamed of you, taking advantage of me like that."

"I'm surprised you showed yourself against the sky."

"It's the damn glasses. I'm stumbling around in the dark. I hadn't realized the sun was that far up yet."

"Liar." I hadn't seen any hint of protective goggles.

"It's getting colder out here, I swear it," came the soft voice again, almost caressing now with promise of better things. "Let's call it quits. We can settle this later."

An old tin can crunched underfoot. I bent down and pried off the lid. The slight silvery sheen remaining after so many years of exposure to the harsh desert environment would be adequate for what I had in mind. I carefully held the lid between my fingers as I poked it up over the edge of the lava rock.

"That's the first logical thing you've said," I called out. I shoved the lid up a bit further.

"Gotcha!" came the triumphant cry. I sensed rather than felt or saw the laser beam strike dead center on the lid.

I said nothing. But I didn't remain in position, either. On feet as soft as any cat's, I moved into a small canyon, then worked my way back uphill. My scouting had shown the main trail led to a box canyon. I waited for my chance.

"Nick! You tricked me."

"You said you wanted to call a truce," I countered and tossed a small rock—a very small one—far down the main trail. Overdoing it at this point would unravel my carefully woven trap.

An amorphous shape worked down the main trail. I aimed carefully, looking for the telltale silver medallions. None cast back the slightest reflection. I cursed under my breath. Not only didn't my would-be assassin wear the protective goggles, the silver dollar-sized medallions were either ripped off or hidden under dirt.

I didn't have a good shot. I waited.

When sure of my position, I slipped back onto the main trail. To get by me required more than skill now—it'd take wings. The walls of the descending canyon were steep. The cul de sac had only one exit and I blocked it with my laser rifle. I closed in for the kill.

"Nick!" came the call from ahead. "Where are you, you sneaky devil? Don't make this any more difficult than it has to be. Admit it now. I'm the winner. I'm the best man."

I tossed another pebble as hard as I could in a perfect parabolic arc. The tiny stone clattered somewhere down the trail. It didn't matter where. It kept attention pulled directly away from my position as I crept closer and closer. If the target medallions weren't easily visible, I had to get near enough to see them. The sun moving higher in the sky helped, but it'd be noon before the full rays found the floor of this dead-end canyon.

I wanted to be out of here and on my way back to base long before then.

"Nick!" This time the call came, sharp, commanding.

The dark form stood exposed ahead of me. I dropped to a kneeling position, brought the laser up, sighted and fired for the head. I missed and the figure spun.

"How'd you get behind me?"

"Never was in front of you," I said, choosing my target carefully. I fired and was rewarded with a tiny yelp. "Did I get an arm, a hand, which is it?"

"Damn you!"

"An arm," I decided out loud. My position was defensible. All that remained was the killing shot.

"Only my left arm," came the reply. The shadow figure moved to the right. I followed. A sudden glint off one of the silvered medallions gave me a target. I fired. Accurately.

"Bastard!"

"That took out your rifle, didn't it?"

"Yes," came the sly reply. The tone hinted at a lie, possibly an attempt to lure me into a trap. Or it could mean I'd been successful and this was only a ploy to buy time. We played a game of not only lies, but half-truths. Either could work. No matter what was said, it was said to win.

"I'm sure of it," I said, rising and slowly walking down the rocky trail. If I had missed, a laser beam would find my body, my head. No ruby lance lashed out.

"Bastard!" came the repeated cry.

I closed and found my assailant trying to climb up the sheer wall of the canyon. Without climbing equipment, the attempt had to end in failure. Not even a spider could make it up the sheer face without a lot of help from somewhere. I stood, rifle cradled gently in the crook of my left arm.

Slipping, almost falling, the bane of my mission turned and glared at me.

"Bastard!" she sneered.

"You aren't as good as you thought, Elaine. Your makeup is smudged," I said softly.

"Go to hell!"

I raised the laser, aimed and fired. The beam struck her directly in the middle of her chest.

TWO

The small campfire still warmed more than the chary, meek sun, now a full ten degrees above the horizon. The coffee I'd brewed helped warm me even more.

"Sure you don't want a cup, Elaine?" I asked, turning to the woman huddled on the far side of the fire.

"No." The single word came out, sullen and tinged with enough bleakness to make me feel a bit guilty.

"It's all just a game, an exercise," I said, trying to cheer her up.

"You can afford to look at it that way. You won."

"Ah, the bet." I couldn't help but smile. Back at AXE headquarters on Dupont Circle in Washington, D.C., Elaine Thompson and I had gotten word of being assigned to this training maneuver in the Arizona desert outside of Tucson. Neither of us had liked the idea. Training is for recruits. We were both seasoned professionals. To take some of the sting out of our "durance vile" we had decided on a small wager. Determining the winner had become easier when we learned of the nature of the training exercise.

I'd been the attacker, Elaine the defender. It had been my mission to take the special laser rifle and plink away at the silver medallions on the convoy trucks and the soldiers guarding them. Every laser touch on a rifle deactivated it. A hit on one of the medallions inflicted a "wound" ranging from a lost arm to death. It was all recorded electronically so there couldn't be any cheating. This made the wargames just a little more realistic and even added a hint of danger to keep everyone honest. The thick goggles were necessary to keep an accidental laser shot from burning a hole in the victim's retina, leaving a permanent blind spot—or even total blindness in that eye.

With a minimal number of shots, I'd hit the sensitized medallions on the trucks, disabling them. And then I'd followed through by taking out fully ten of the soldiers. With the laser, it had been far easier than if I'd had to rely on a high-powered rifle. The range had been extreme for a bullet. But this small element of beneficial unreality for me had been offset by the exercise's planners.

Elaine had been assigned to track me down, without being told what constituted success for my portion of the mission. From a mission standpoint, stopping the convoy had been adequate. From a personal one, getting away without being "killed" constituted real triumph. It made it more like an actual field assignment with life and death riding on the outcome.

I'm sure that's the way David Hawk, my boss at AXE, planned it.

"I'd have had you, Nick," she said bitterly. "I would have!"

"But you didn't. I think you were cheating a bit, too. I didn't see you wearing the protective goggles. And your target medallions were suspiciously dirty." She smiled and I forgave her attempts to cheat.

Elaine Thompson wasn't a beautiful woman, but there was a glow about her, a vitality that appealed greatly to me. Perhaps because we were in the same business we had shared goals and drives. Ego keeps all of us going back into the field, accepting more and more impossible assignments, pushing ourselves to the limits of our abilities. We have to prove ourselves constantly. Between Elaine and me there was obvious competition, but there was also recognition of our inner needs.

We understood what motivated the other.

Elaine pushed back her light brown hair to reveal a broad forehead, delicately sculpted eyebrows and eyes that

now seemed like pools of melted chocolate. The firelight
danced and highlighted her soft facial features. The pink
tip of her tongue emerged from between lips and made a
slow, wet, sensuous circuit. With another woman, I
would have wondered if she realized she did it. Everything
Elaine did was calculated. Under the soft exterior worked
a cool, deliberate mind.

"It's getting warm," she said, shedding her jacket. The
medallions clanked as she discarded the Army field jacket
with its electronics. She wore a soft flannel shirt. Her
breasts weren't large, but they filled the shirt well. I saw the
slight sway as she moved, indicating she hadn't burdened
herself with a bra. Even as I watched, nipples hardened
and pressed into the warm cotton fabric.

"Do you remember that time in Rio?" I asked. "It was
the middle of summer and the Nazi death camp commander had finally come out of hiding in the jungles."

"He had a place somewhere up on the Orinoco, didn't
he?" she asked, her eyes unfocusing slightly as she remembered. "I said I'd do anything to be cool. I felt as if I was
ready to melt down into a blob of undifferentiated proto-
plasm at any instant."

"This is nowhere near as hot."

She snorted. A tiny plume of her breath formed and
gusted away the instant the sunlight struck it. The temperature was climbing substantially even as we sat and
reminisced.

"My ideal climate is close to the old Greek idea. The
Golden Mean. Not too much of anything. Not too hot, not
too cold. Maybe around sixty-five, never over seventy."

"It might get dull if the temperature didn't vary," I
pointed out. I took a drink of the coffee. Somehow it tasted
better, in spite of being boiled over a campfire. Maybe it
tasted better because of that. "Things staying the same get
boring after a while."

"Everything, Nick?" she asked, her eyes brighter than
ever.

"Maybe not *everything*," I conceded, knowing what she
meant.

"Winning is always a rush, a high drugs never come close to matching," Elaine said, sighing. "And there are other things, too."

"I can think of one, right off the top of my head," I said. Her gaze fastened on mine. I didn't have to explain what I meant. We both knew.

"The bet?" she asked.

"You're not going to deliver, are you?" I asked, my voice low.

"It wasn't a very fair bet, after all. You've used the laser rifles before in training. Remember when you worked with the men on the squad guarding the atomic weapons shipments? They used the laser rifles, and you got pretty damn good with them."

"One weapon is like another. These just don't kill."

She stood. Her hips were firm, womanly, her waist slender. Elaine Thompson, like all AXE agents, stayed in superb physical condition. The tight jeans she wore clung to her firm thighs and slender legs.

"You had unfair advantage, Nick. You had been told the rules beforehand. I came out here blind."

"Blind? I was the one wearing the goggles. One stray shot from that laser rifle will blind you. And who dirtied up her targets so I wouldn't have a clear shot?"

"I'm not going to pay off on the bet!" she cried. "Not now. Never!" With a leap like a frightened gazelle, she hurtled the fire, pushed hard against my shoulders and sent me rolling backward. The move didn't catch me entirely off guard. I went with the shove, rolled and came to my feet just beyond the fire.

"Yes, you will. Now!" I said emphatically.

Elaine not only leaped like a gazelle, she ran like one. The woman took off with a speed that any Olympic sprinter would envy. I shucked off my jacket and bolted after her. She dodged, darted and eluded me, but I was faster. I herded her around until her back was against a stone canyon wall. We'd come almost a hundred yards from camp.

"Now," I said, advancing on her. "Now you're going to pay off."

She was expert in hand-to-hand combat; I was better.
The first thrust of her slender hand aimed deadly fingers
for my throat. I turned the blow aside and stepped inside
the circle of her arms. She drove an elbow down into my
shoulder. It hurt like hell but I wasn't about to let it stop me
now.

My hands shot forward, both slipping into the neckline
of the flannel shirt. A quick movement, a good grip, then I
yanked. The movement forced her up onto her toes. In this
position, she couldn't effectively fight me. She had to stay
exactly where she was until I released my grip.

"Bastard!" she cried. She got one foot up onto a stone
for balance, robbing my grip of its effectiveness. As she
tried to kick me in the groin, I turned and took her knee on
the side of my thigh. I held onto her shirt and pulled it
back, buttons sailing all over the ravine, trapping her arms
at her sides.

A quick move spun her around. She arched away from
the rough lava rock to keep from scraping her sensitive
breasts on the stone. I used this backward thrusting of her
rump to my advantage. Not wanting her to run away again
wasn't enough on my part. I had to act.

Her jeans pulled down around her ankles. Elaine
Thompson was now effectively trapped, her arms pinned
by her shirt and legs by tough denim.

"I'll get you for this, Nick, I will!" she cried.

"And now you're going to pay off. You lost the bet. I
won. Now I'm going to collect."

"Bastard!" she shrieked.

I fumbled around until I found her pants pocket. Her
kicking thwarted my first efforts to reach into the pocket
but I finally succeeded. A few coins tumbled out into the
palm of my hand. Fishing out the dime that constituted the
entire bet, I put the rest back into her pocket.

"Now I'm satisfied," I said. The amount didn't matter. It
could have been a million dollars instead of a dime and the
effort we both put into this training mission and its after-
math would have been the same. The winning counted,
and that couldn't be measured in dimes or dollars.

"Nick," she said, her voice low and choked with emotion.

"What?"

"Carry me back to camp. Please."

This surprised me. Elaine never said "please" under any circumstances. Or so I'd thought.

I spun her around and hoisted her up and over my shoulder, her behind next to my head.

"Nick!" she protested. "Not like this! I meant . . ."

I started back to the campfire at a trot. She bounced up and down, her arms and legs still encumbered. Elaine struggled weakly, then desisted until we reached the warming blaze. I kicked a couple more sticks of dried mesquite wood onto the fire, then put the woman down.

She stood before me, jeans around her ankles and her flannel shirt dangling by her wrists. Elaine dropped the shirt and stepped out of the jeans. Her boots followed. The combination of light from the sun and the fire gave her a primitive, nymphlike appearance. She might have been a female spirit sent to seduce me.

"Nick," she said in a voice husky with promise.

"Yes, Elaine."

"Do you know what I'd have asked for if I'd've won?"

I didn't answer. She hadn't said what my penalty would have been if she'd won. I'd only told her of what I wanted if she lost the bet. She stepped forward and knelt in front of me. Her hands gently undid my shirt, my belt, my trousers. As she worked I kicked out of my boots. Arms around each other we silently went into the small puptent I'd pitched. My sleeping bag stretched out invitingly. The coolness of the desert morning had chilled both of our bodies; our passions kept us warm.

We crawled into the sleeping bag. It was snug, but somehow we barely noticed. Our mouths met in silent communion. The kiss deepened and our tongues began darting back and forth.

"*Ummm*, Nick, this is so nice. Better than I thought it would be."

"Why do we have to be so aloof, so distant?" I mur-

mured in Elaine's shell-like ear. Our job instilled a certain distrust and paranoia about the motives of others. Even other AXE agents were viewed with suspicion.

It never pays to get too close. Betrayal can come from any quarter. Even worse, get too friendly with someone and then feel the pain and loss when they don't come back from a mission. The distance in AXE helps. But sometimes it makes for a lonely job.

"It's hell. But this is different, Nick."

"Different how?" I asked, smiling.

"This is what we both need now, Nick darling."

And she was right. It's always been a puzzle to me why close brushes with death, the completion of a mission, the feeling of doing what no other can do increases the sex drive. It does with me, and I was finding out firsthand that it did for Elaine, too.

I moaned softly as her hand worked down the hardness of my muscled belly, down lower to another hardness. She took me in hand and pulled me even closer. Her breasts mashed flat against my chest. I felt the throbbing points of her nipples trying to poke holes in my chest. Our mouths locked firmly together again. Then her legs parted.

With a smooth motion, I surged forward. She gasped, then lifted her behind enough for complete entry. Surrounded by clinging, hot, damp female flesh, I felt as if I'd died and gone to heaven.

Elaine Thompson was a complex person. All AXE agents have to be. Bright, competent, she was one of the best AXE had. Her record spoke for itself. Few agents have done better. What drove her in the field? Why did she go for the hardest assignments, then come back for more? What lure did danger have for her?

As her nails clawed at my back, as I felt her responding more and more strongly, I got a flash of telepathic communication unique during lovemaking. Understanding Elaine was simple. She wore a hard shell around her to keep from getting hurt, physically or emotionally. Somehow, I'd penetrated that shell, at least for a short while. We could share, be equal, not be rivals.

I began moving with smooth, easy strokes that drove her into a frenzy of desire. We melted together and became one. My knees pressed down through the sleeping bag against the hard earth. Using this as leverage, I rose up slightly. She peaked then.

"N-Nick!" she groaned out. Her fingernails raked my back. I ignored the sharp pain and bent down and kissed her breasts, nibbling at the hard points, working on the coppery-colored bumpy plains surrounding them.

My movements began to be more insistent, more powerful. The passions rising inside me couldn't be held back. As much as Elaine, I needed this lovemaking. My fingers stroked down the smooth flanks, past the trim waist and finally curled under the white cheeks moving so smoothly to the rhythm of her inner needs.

I thrust and moved and finally went over the brink myself.

Afterward, we lay in my sleeping bag, arms around each other. She snuggled close, her head under my chin. I felt hot, gusty breathing caress my chest.

"You've got a lot of scars, Nick," she said.

"So do you."

"I do not! Well, the one on my leg."

"I didn't mean physically." She tensed. I didn't allow her to pull away.

"You see too much, Nick. Maybe that's why you're Hawk's top agent."

"He doesn't play favorites," I said. And Hawk didn't. He was the fairest man I knew. Logic, not emotion, dictated when he handed out assignments. I'd gotten some missions that looked like real plums to others in the department. I'd gotten them because I was the best choice for them, not because Hawk liked me.

If it came down to brass tacks, Hawk put the job before the person. I tried to emulate that attitude. It was one I appreciated.

"That's not what I'm talking about. You don't want to hear my life story, yet you seem to know it."

Unhappy marriage, an unfaithful lover, I didn't know

what Elaine's life history was like. All I knew was that the woman in my arms feared involvement on any permanent basis. The lovemaking had been a physical release for me; it opened the floodgates of her psyche. And now those gates were closing, shutting out all other humans, me included. She was complete unto herself and couldn't live any other way.

Maybe that was why I felt drawn to her. I recognized that as being a part of my own mindset, too.

"I see the results."

"So do I," she said, grinning up at me. Her hand had been working between my legs. Life stirred again.

As I rolled over atop her again, pain lanced into my left shoulder. I winced. There wasn't any hiding it from her.

"Hawk?" she asked.

"Yes, dammit. I wish to hell I didn't have that communicator buried in my shoulder." Whenever Hawk wanted me—fast—he simply pressed a button on his desk. An electronic signal shot up to one of the AXE satellites, then was relayed back to the receiving unit buried in my shoulder. A sharp, harmless pain told me I was wanted. Immediately.

"Do we have time?" Elaine asked.

The beating of the helicopter rotors outside answered her question. Reluctantly, I crawled from the sleeping bag and dressed. Thirty minutes later, a jet took me toward Washington, D.C., at twice the speed of sound.

THREE

The blue cloud of smoke from Hawk's cigar almost choked me. I'd been out in the clear, pure air of the desert too long. The only way possible to combat breathing the air polluted by that thick cigar smoke was to add a bit of pollution of my own. I took out my gold cigarette case, tapped out a monogrammed cigarette and lit it. The smoke gusted through my lungs, relaxing me and sending tiny messages of delight coursing along my nerve-endings.

It wasn't as good as clean air, but it was better than Hawk's smelly cigar.

"You did well on this training mission, Nick," the man said. David Hawk looked forty-five or so, but I knew he had to be in his late fifties. He kept remarkably trim for someone holding down a desk job in Washington. Through the years, I'd seldom caught him away from his post. And when I had, he'd been in a high-level conference. Very high level, usually with the President. Unlike a lot of his fellows in similar positions, he never showed the stress except for his habitual gnawing and chewing at the cigar stub. Watching that was almost worse than enduring the cloying miasma as it burned.

"Thank you, sir," I said, exhaling a lungful of cigarette smoke. I watched it drift out and mingle with the smoke hanging like an LA smog over the desk. "It was a nice diversion."

"It was a serious training exercise, N3," he said sternly.

"My record speaks for itself. I don't need periodic reevaluation."

"You weren't sent out there for reevaluation. I wanted you to learn desert survival techniques. I wanted you to appreciate the difficulties of a mission where there might not be much water, where the animals and plants and bugs are all potential dangers."

"The Arizona desert isn't that dangerous. I didn't even see a rattlesnake. As to climate . . ." I shrugged. It had been cold at night and hot in the day, but it was winter. I'd survived worse. And I'd survive worse in the future.

"Granted, there aren't the deserts in the U.S. that can push you to the limit."

"But there are deserts that will, somewhere in the world?"

"In Australia."

I frowned. Australia hardly seemed the place for an AXE agent to be sent. This was friendly territory, virtually home base for United States concerns. All we had to do, in most things, was to ask the Australians and they cooperated. AXE handles the hard cases, the dangerous ones requiring a light touch, sure decisions, swift action. The CIA has its place. They engage in intelligence gathering more than clandestine activities, in spite of all the bad press they receive about their ill-conceived covert missions. The other intelligence gathering branches work parallel to the CIA—the Defense Nuclear Agency, Defense Intelligence Agency, National Security Agency and the rest of the Washington alphabet soup of spook groups.

They gather, we act. It's a nice arrangement since we're all doing what we do best.

But Australia?

"I see you are skeptical, N3. Let me give you some background."

The lights dimmed and a picture of the President hanging on the far wall began to fade in its cherry-wood frame. Replacing the smiling face appeared a picture of a spy satellite, complete with lenses bulging out and an array of communications antennas looking like an explosion in a wire coat hanger factory.

"A VELA satellite?" I asked.

"Yes, Nick. One of the Defense Department's. Officially it's a weather satellite, but it performs other duties."

"Over Australia?"

"Over most of the South Pacific several times a day since it's in a polar orbit. It picked up Soviet activity off the coast of the Philippines almost a year ago. We checked."

"The mission Morris had?" I asked. Hawk glowered at me. Another agent's assignments weren't discussed. In fact, I wasn't supposed to even know of it. But in any organization—perhaps especially in a group of spies trained to ferret out information—word gets around. Morris had gone into the Philippines and eliminated a Russian installation. I hadn't heard any more details.

"The Soviets have become bolder in placing clandestine radar stations in countries friendly to the U.S. Morris removed the one in the Philippines; others have been eliminated in India, Japan and Sri Lanka. This is a photo of one of the units."

The satellite left the picture frame and was replaced by a pretty standard looking Russian radar installation. The equipment looked like off-the-shelf stuff, nothing special to get worked up about. Knowing that Hawk never handed out assignments without good reason, there had to be more to this than met the eye.

I puffed on my cigarette, thinking about what Hawk said. Radar stations in those countries wouldn't help us any. The Soviets could monitor all activity in the Indian Ocean, an area increasingly important to our security.

"The bases were difficult to detect. The spy satellites have adequate 'look-down' ability for most things, but these sites were camouflaged well. We were lucky in all cases and caught the Russians actually establishing the bases."

I nodded. The satellites took great pictures. A newspaper headline was visible—and readable—from the cameras aboard, but detecting the operation of a radar station after all the equipment was up and running might be too much to ask. The satellites were good but they weren't omniscient. In fact, even detecting low-flying, fast-moving airplanes pushed their capabilities to the limit. The satellite over Saudi Arabia had missed entirely the flight of Israeli F-4 Phantoms on their way to bomb the nuclear reactor in Iraq.

That had sparked Saudi interest in our AWACS surveillance planes. The Russians obviously couldn't put up recon planes of their own, so they sneaked in entire radar units and hid them under our noses. Neat.

And treacherous.

"They monitor not only our flights, but the flights of our allies. They are able to check on down-range test firings from China, in addition to their own Pacific impact launches. Of course, the Australian launches from Woomera are an open book to them. The ELDO missile system is still being tested there. It will not do having the Russians know more about it than we do, since the Australians are rather closed-mouthed concerning it."

Hawk leaned back and stared at the radar installation as if his life depended on memorizing every little detail. I suspect he already had memorized it; it was my life that depended on the details.

I considered how easily the Russians could monitor those ELDO launches from Woomera. This particular missile system had been one of those peculiar Anglo-French collaborations designed to show the Third World it was possible to build their very own ICBM. From all accounts, the French second stage of the rocket malfunctioned regularly, but the Australians continued testing. They'd been at it so long, I wondered if it hadn't become a matter of pride in completing it rather than defense necessity or common sense.

Hawk's cigar finally went out, leaving only a short stub. He didn't seem to notice. He actively moved the stub from one side of his mouth to the other as he talked.

"Something that we consider to be even worse for national security, such radar bases allow the Soviets to accurately guide in their own missiles in case of war."

"That means they don't have to develop more sophisticated guidance techniques," I said. The Russians always sought new ways of circumventing our lead in microelectronics and computers. A cheap, standard radar unit at the target site eliminated the need for complex and expensive inertial guidance systems.

"They can also home in their surface vessels. Since a radar site is difficult to detect in operation, we're having problems finding one already established."

"You've mentioned Japan, the Philippines and so forth. Those were caught in the process of being built?"

"Yes. And we've missed entirely the one in Australia."

I didn't ask Hawk how he knew one existed there. A dozen channels existed for such intelligence to be passed along. It might even be CIA information.

"Where is it located?" I asked, thinking this would be a small demolition job and nothing more.

"We don't know, N3. That's your mission. Find and destroy it."

FOUR

"'Find and destroy it,' he says," I muttered as I pored over maps of Australia. The damn continent was as large as the United States, had a tenth the population huddled in a necklace of fertile land around the coast and sported an eleven hundred by twelve hundred mile rectangle of desert in the center.

One point thirty-two million square miles of desert. And on about two hundred square feet of that terrain huddled a Soviet radar station. The proverbial needle in a haystack looked like a simple problem in comparison.

At least with the needle, you could magnetize it or make it radioactive. All I had going for me was the notion that the Russians were probably complacent thinking their handiwork was well hidden. What galled me the most was that they were right.

I leaned back in the upholstered chair and took a deep drag off my cigarette. The AXE library surrounding me was one of the finest in the world. Agents required up-to-the-minute details on a wild variety of topics. The dozen full-time librarians were entrusted with keeping lines of information open constantly.

I went back to my book on Australia. I didn't think I'd get much from it and I was right. The feel was wrong. There wasn't any way of experiencing the problems I'd encounter only by reading a book. My feet hoisted onto the low table in front of the chair. If nothing else, AXE made sure that their agents were comfortable here. It was a place to think as much as to read and learn.

Something didn't ring true about this assignment. Hawk didn't waste my talents on trivial matters. Granted, finding the radar station didn't seem to be a trivial problem, but AXE already had an agent on the scene. I glanced at the dossier opened and lying in my lap.

Sanford Marian.

That made the problem even more peculiar. Marian was a good man. Not too long ago he had pulled the fat out of the fire for a half dozen undercover agents in the Far East. By taking out a KGB informer, he had earned himself a commendation and the eternal gratitude of four men and two women. Prior to that, he'd done good work in a variety of assignments. While he wasn't considered top of the line, first-rate material, he was competent.

Competent in AXE's jargon meant excellent in any other agency.

"Why doesn't Marian handle this by himself?" I wondered aloud.

"May I help you, sir?" came the quiet, efficient tones of a woman. I glanced over my shoulder. One of the librarians had overheard my chance comment.

"No, everything's okay. Just thinking out loud." I studied the woman more carefully. She wore a typical frowsy librarian's dress and had her hair severely pulled up into a bun. The dark-framed glasses made her look like an owl. Yet underneath this disguise hid a pretty woman. The bone structure was nice and the way she moved hinted at a model's grace.

"Are you sure, sir?"

"Are you sure you're a librarian?" I asked.

"Why?"

"The hair coloring is wrong. With four-inch high heels, a different dress and no glasses you'd be a dead ringer for an agent in South America, that's why."

She laughed and smiled broadly.

"I told the Special Effects Department they couldn't fool you. This is a sample of their new makeup for field agents.

I'm testing it out for them while I recuperate."

I didn't ask what injuries she'd had. In fact, I didn't even remember her name. All I knew was that I'd seen her face before. No amount of makeup, gross or subtle, prevented me from getting to the heart of the real person.

"So you're not actually a librarian?"

"Afraid not. But if you like, I can get one."

"Find one who knows about Australian wildlife."

"Right. And, thanks."

Just watching her walk away was thanks enough. I was sorry I hadn't gotten her name, but in our ranks names don't matter too much. And it didn't pay to get too attached to anyone. That was my problem, that was Elaine Thompson's problem, that was every agent's problem. Get involved and someone dies. The psychic pain can be too much—or it can permanently harden.

I preferred not to get involved. I wanted to believe human feelings still existed somewhere deep inside me, if I should ever need them.

A woman in her late forties came up and asked, "What do you wish to know about flora and fauna in Australia, Mr. Carter?"

My mental filing cabinet flashed through thousands of pictures; I'd seen this woman before, too. She'd been awarded the Lasker Prize for medical research some years back. She was an expert in her field. And she spent time here in the library. I wondered what inducements had been used. Possibly unlimited research facilities in exchange for her expertise.

"What poisonous animals am I likely to run into in Australia? The place seems like a leftover from the Ice Age."

"Snakes," she said, simply. Her watery eyes had a far-off look in them.

"So I'd better wear high-topped boots."

She laughed, startling me.

"I'm sorry, Mr. Carter. Only the 'new chums' bother with such boots."

"'New chums?'"

"Those new to the bush. One variety of brown snake is able to leap over head-high. The cobra's bite is sufficient to kill thirty sheep, the tiger snake's venom will kill over a hundred and a single bite from a taipan snake is twice as deadly as that."

"Remind me to stay in the water away from all those."

"Sorry, sir, but the water snakes are even more dangerous. There is no recorded survivor of a bite from a northern water snake." The eyes glazed over again and a wistful smile came to her lips. "They swarm until they look like spaghetti in the water. Thousands of them."

"How charming."

"But this doesn't happen too often."

"Why not?" I asked, playing the game. I wasn't sure I wanted to hear the answer.

"Because of the sharks. The sharks love them for lunch. Or dinner."

"Let me guess. You're an expert on snakes."

"No, sir, I'm the AXE consultant on poisons. Australia happens to be a favorite spot of mine because so many different poisons abound, both in animals and in the plants. The abos—the aborigines—actually have to scour out the poisons from most of what they eat."

She then launched off into a discussion of the fifty thousand species of insects, the thousand species of ants, thirty of which had been brought in by man and any one of which was more dangerous than the prior variety. I hardly believed her description of the *Myrmecia* being an inch and a half long and chasing people, not to mention moving faster than a slow camera shutter can capture. When the grinning expert on poisons finally took her leave, I looked that one up.

She was right. More and more I understood why Sanford Marian didn't want to handle this on his own.

"You look pensive."

Pulled out of my reverie, I peered up. My reactions are all automatic. My right hand half-reached for my Luger, Wilhelmina, holstered under my left arm. I stopped the motion when I recognized Elaine Thompson.

"Back from the desert already?" I asked. "Hawk told me he had run out of money getting me back and had just given you a bus ticket."

"I picked up a MATS flight. Slower than your taxi, but it got me here just in time to be given a new assignment."

"In Australia?" I asked suspiciously. It bordered on the unique if Hawk assigned Elaine there, too. Three agents constituted a major expedition rather than a simple search and destroy.

"Nope," she said, her tone glum. "But close. New Zealand."

I wanted to ask what took her to New Zealand but held back.

She caught my mood and smiled. Elaine had a pair of crooked teeth in front and a slight overbite. Her skin was weathered and tending toward leather after being out on the desert for our little training session, and I wouldn't have given her a second look except for the way her eyes sparkled and danced.

"You want to know why, don't you, Nick?"

"Of course I do. And I'm not asking."

"I'll tell you." Her voice hardened slightly. I caught it immediately. She wasn't happy with the assignment and wanted to gripe about it. "I'm being sent there to do a census on penguins."

I laughed. But the laugh died down. The sour expression on her face didn't change.

"You're serious!"

"I'd think about quitting except that Hawk promised me a better assignment next time around."

"You're going to count penguins?" This struck me as the most tragic waste imaginable. Elaine was extraordinarily intelligent. I hated to rate others against me when they're on my side, but on her best day she might actually be better than I am.

"There's been some Soviet submarine activity off the coast of New Zealand. I'm going down there with a cover of biologist. I'm to sit on deck, count penguins for the National Geographic and try to pick up some info on the sub activity."

"That's not an AXE mission. That's not even a CIA mission. The spy satellites, the sonar buoys used with the Orion picket planes, the . . ." I sputtered as the woman's words sank in even more fully.

"Nick," she said in a soft voice, "you're not saying a word I haven't already said to Hawk."

"And still you're going." That wasn't a question, it was a statement. Hawk has an incredibly devious mind. She had to be working on some other chore.

"I've got my camera and binoculars packed and that's it."

Her personal weapons weren't mentioned. There wasn't any need. I never went anywhere without my trusty Wilhelmina, Hugo, so lovingly sheathed on my forearm, or Pierre, the tiny gas pellet hidden in an imitation skin pouch on my inner right thigh. Elaine Thompson had her own companions.

"What other instructions?"

"None."

I sank into the softness of the chair and studied the woman. None of the signs, the subtle messages of body language, gave even a hint that she lied. A superb actress can hide some from a trained observer, and Elaine was certainly well-schooled in deception, but the set of her mouth, the involuntary tightness around her eyes, the way a muscle spasmodically jerked in her throat, those and a hundred other signs I wasn't consciously aware of, all told me how incensed she was over this.

I applied some heavy thinking to the problem. Elaine Thompson was topnotch. This wasn't a punishment assignment for her. Other agencies do that; AXE can't afford to waste personnel. We're either good enough for a real mission or we're canned. Period. Penguin watching didn't constitute a real mission.

Hawk can't afford to waste personnel. That thought came back to me, but it turned over in different ways in my mind, different meanings forming.

"What sort of contact are you supposed to maintain with AXE headquarters?"

"The usual."

That meant Elaine would be only seconds away from a direct order from Hawk, no matter where either was in the world.

"And how long would it take you to get to Australia from this boat out in the Antarctic Ocean?"

She shrugged. "Days, a week? I don't know."

"To hell with it, Elaine," I said. "I'm slated for Australia."

"The desert?" she asked. Her entire body seemed to fold in upon itself.

"Yeah," I answered.

"That's it, then. We were out on the training mission. You won and I lost. You get the cushy assignment and this is Hawk's way of telling me to do better next time."

I didn't tell her I'd already discarded that idea. Instead, I slammed shut the book on the table, carefully closed the dossier and put it back into a briefcase and turned to face her.

"If I'm in for a cushy assignment in the Australian desert, it's news to me after listening to all the horror tales about the bugs and snakes there. But if I won and you lost, you deserve a consolation prize."

"Dinner?" Elaine said, brightening.

"At least. Then perhaps some dancing."

"C&W?"

"I didn't know you were the goat-roper type. But yes, country and western dancing."

"And then, Nick?" she asked, her voice soft and her gaze bold.

"Then we'll see."

It was a great send-off for me, even if I was tired from our lovemaking when I boarded the jet that would fly me halfway around the world. Elaine would follow in a week— for New Zealand. It'd be quite some time before our paths crossed again.

Maybe.

FIVE

I'd picked up a ride in an SR-71 Blackbird from Andrews AFB to the West Coast. From there I hitched a ride on a military jet transport to Hickam Field in Hawaii, got the chance to see a momentary flash of the sunlight and white beaches and was off again on still another plane, this time a dilapidated C-47 cargo prop. I felt groggy by the time the flight master came back and shook me.

I'd tried to doze and hadn't been too successful. The weather over the South Pacific was anything but peaceful. The plane rocked and buffeted from strong headwinds, and the rapid changing of time zones really hit me hard. I had no feeling at all for what time it was. My Rolex said one thing, my body another.

"Time to leave," the man said.

I peered up at him through bloodshot eyes. A full twenty hours of flying isn't the best start on a friendship, not that I wanted even small talk from the burly master sergeant. As flight master it was his responsibility to get rid of surplus cargo whenever the time was right. I had to take his word that it was my turn to go.

"Already?" I said. "Seems like l just got here."

"The party was dying, anyway," the man said, slinging a heavy parachute around and tossing it to me. I fielded it and began working my arms and legs into the webbed nylon straps. The next part didn't please me at all, but Hawk had assured me it was the quickest way of getting into Australia.

I had to believe him, even if I didn't like it.

"Go when the light turns green," the flight master said.

I glanced up and saw a baleful red light winking on and off. The sergeant had snapped a D-ring running to my ripcord to the static line overhead. Shaking my head, I undid his handiwork. In weather like this I wanted to time it exactly when my chute opened. I shuffled forward, toes just over the edge of the doorway. I looked down into the choppy, turbulent waters of the Pacific. More men had gone down there never to be seen again than could be listed. It took a complete fool to want to jump into the frothy, churning, heaving ten-foot waves.

The light turned green. I jumped.

The wind caught me the instant I stepped out of the plane. At first I thought it was only propwash from the engines, but when it continued I knew firsthand just how potent the headwind we'd fought actually was. I twisted and turned, pulling my hands back to my sides. This pointed my head downward.

A small storm worked its way across the horizon, coming in my direction. The leading edge of the front buffeted me around until I felt as if I'd lose control and begin tumbling. I reached forward and fiddled with the dials on my chestpack. A light turned from red to amber to green as I watched. When it flashed amber, I extended arms and legs and maneuvered in mid-air until the green returned.

This homing device was all that would keep me alive in the storm. If I landed too far from the submarine sent to pick me up, my name would be added to the list of those nameless sailors who had been swallowed whole by the misnamed Pacific.

Damn Balboa for thinking this ocean was in the least peaceful.

When my altimeter read one thousand feet, I pulled the ripcord. For a heartstopping instant. fear raced through me. Would the chute open? The hard jerk that dropped me feet-first told the tale. But the rush of adrenaline remained. I savored the heightened senses, the quickened pulse, the way life felt more real, more dear than ever. Then I was underwater, struggling to the rolling surface, trying to get free of the entangling shroud lines.

The quick-releases got me out of my harness, but I fought constantly to keep my head above water. The mountains of waves on all sides looked like the Himalayas to me. Without the proper gear, I'd never live to scale even the smallest of those wet peaks.

"Noooo!" I shrieked as something hard and powerful struck my legs. The vision of a shark came instantly to mind. Those snapping jaws, the voracious appetite, the need for sustenance—human flesh, *my* flesh—were pictured all too vividly before I realized that my legs were still firmly attached to my body. In fact, I was being lifted up and out of the water. The waves were dwindling in size and were soon below my line of sight.

The cold, implacable steel deck of the submarine had never felt more comfortable.

I rolled over and spit out a mouthful of water. Sitting up, shaking myself like a dog, I saw a nearby hatch open and a white-capped head poking out. The expression on the seaman's face told me he didn't like being on deck in weather like this.

"Mr. Carter?" the rating called. "Will you please come below? The captain's waiting for you."

"Be glad to join him. This isn't any kind of a day to walk my dog."

"Not even if it's a dogfish, sir," he said, smiling.

I said nothing. Such jocularity in the face of wet and cold and wind was its own punishment. I scrambled below, leaving a giant wet spot on the floor where my clothes dripped from my little swim. I pulled off the heavy canvas bag containing the electronic homing gear. It had served its purpose. No need to keep it any longer.

"This way, sir. You can change in Commander Goble's quarters. He's our exec." He held back a curtain and waited until I'd gone in. The small cubicle differed greatly from the quarters aboard an atomic-powered submarine. These were cramped to the point of requiring me to walk in and back out. I found a nondescript set of clothes that fit me well enough to be presentable to the boat's captain. Drying off, warming up and changing clothes did a world of good for my morale. The bone-weariness from the long trip still haunted me, but it wasn't anything a few hours of sack time wouldn't cure.

The sailor patiently waited outside the door for me, then ushered me into the captain's quarters. The man, stocky, well-built, a little gray at the temples and cold, calculating blue eyes stood as I came in.

"Mr. Carter," he said without preamble. "I'm Captain Horvat. Be seated. This is most unusual," he went on, glancing over a sheet of flimsy paper. The light shone through it enough to allow me to catch phrases here and there. What I saw made me smile. This may have been the first time a simple submarine commander had received an order directly from the admiral on the Joint Chiefs of Staff.

"My mission is of the highest priority," I said. In a way, that flimsy bothered me. Everything Hawk had told me about the mission said it was difficult, possibly a tad on the dangerous side, but nothing compared to others I'd undertaken in previous years. To pull out the big guns—the Joint Chiefs—to get me onto the submarine taking me to Australia seemed like overkill.

I worried about what Hawk hadn't told me.

The nearness of Elaine Thompson in New Zealand, the heavy use of military connections, the desert training, all that was too much for a simple search and destroy mission on a Russian radar station. Sure, the radar unit posed real danger—but only in the case of war. Until then, it was nothing more than an information drain sucking up details on overflights, missile tests and other military goodies. Irritating but not top of the line priority.

I worried even more.

"My orders are unequivocable," Captain Horvat went on. "You are to receive every courtesy, I'm to get you to the SS Constance bound for Sydney, and I am to ask no questions."

"But you want to ask, don't you?" I said.

The man's cold eyes bored into me. He obviously didn't

care to be at the mercy of a civilian, especially one dropping in from out of the sky carrying orders from the Joint Chiefs of Staff. I had no idea what his mission was out here in the Pacific, but he obviously thought it important. And it probably was. By disturbing his patrol area, he felt I endangered U.S. security.

Maybe I did. All I could do was follow my own strict orders.

"I would like to grab a little sleep before we rendezvous with the cruise ship."

"Cruise ship?" he asked. His eyebrows shot up. "The *SS Constance* is a goddamn cruise ship?" He slammed a meaty fist onto his desk and settled back, glowering at me. I was glad I wasn't one of his crew on the receiving end of that only-barely contained wrath. He'd mistakenly pegged me as a Congressional thrill-seeker highly connected in the Pentagon who was using a U.S. Navy submarine on patrol duty as a limousine service to board a luxury liner.

I didn't correct the impression. All I wanted was a few hours sleep. Captain Horvat was glad to give me that, though he did look at me with daggers in his eyes when I insisted on sneaking aboard the *Constance* after dark and without anyone spotting the sub. Visions of illicit assignations and love nests and who knows what else ran through his mind.

I wished he'd been right.

No one knew I was aboard the cruise ship. I spent the little time available leaning over the railing, waiting to round the coastline that would put us into Sydney Harbor. Getting through customs was going to be easy enough for me. All I had with me was a battered suitcase filled with innocuous clothing. My weapons waited for me in Sydney. I doubted anyone on the ship would question my miraculous appearance. The crew hadn't seen me come aboard and with over a thousand passengers, what was one more strange face.

Coming in, the ship passed through the Heads, those

looming, craggy cliffs that break the fierce Antarctic Ocean storms pounding the continent in the "winter" months of July and August. One passage a few hundred yards across leads from the ship-destroying ocean into one of the most beautiful harbors I'd ever seen. The calm waters were blood-warm, and gentle shores turned and twisted into hundreds of bays and inlets. White sandy beach looking more inviting by the second and soft hills furred with a verdant green of the gum trees were dotted with houses all roofed in red tile.

But the tranquility of the setting was belied by the waters around the ship. I remembered what the AXE expert on poisons had said about the sharks. Six species of man-eating sharks indigenous to the harbor circled Shark Island poised in the center of the bay like a wary sentinel. I felt lucky in not having to skydive into this harbor. No amount of turbulent Pacific Ocean matched the appetite of even one shark.

The *Constance* swept past Fort Denison where the original convict-settlers of Australia sweated out their sentences. And I stood and took in the beauty of the Opera House, a series of conch shells vanishing away from the waterfront. When we finally sailed under the steel arc of the Sydney Harbor Bridge hundreds of feet above, we were virtually in the heart of the city itself.

After the routine baggage search, I made my way out into the bright sunlight of Sydney. The warmth seeped into my bones and took away some of the tiredness I felt. Glancing around, I debated my next move. I didn't know this city as well as some others, but I still knew enough to avoid the eastern suburbs laden with prostitutes and the slums in Redfern. The information needed to finish my mission wasn't available in places like that. Rather, I wanted to stay within sight of the harbor.

Perhaps Woollahara or Vaucluse. First I'd establish a base of operation, then meet with Sanford Marian and find out what the hell was going on.

SIX

I sipped at the straight scotch, allowing the pungent liquor to roll over my tongue before softly sliding down my gullet.

I was in the lobby of the hotel I'd found in Rose Bay, less than a quarter mile from the harbor. The sound of the waves gently lapping against the shoreline soothed me, made me relax a bit and forget the paranoid suspicions I had about this mission. Hawk hadn't been honest with me about it. What bothered me even worse was being unable to see through the smoke screen he'd erected and get to the heart of the matter.

"Nick, old chap," greeted Marian. "It's been a while, eh?"

"That is has," I agreed. The only time we'd met had been four years ago in Mexico City. Marian had tracked down an assassin specializing in British Commonwealth ministers; I'd been free and had acted as backup. My services hadn't been necessary. Sanford Marian had made a clean kill with a single shot, distance about two hundred yards. It had been a tricky assignment but one performed with flair and distinction.

"I do so wish Hawk had told me you were coming."

Hiding my bewilderment took all my accumulated skills. Everything Hawk had said had led me to believe that Marian had asked for assistance, perhaps even asking for me specifically.

"Does it surprise you I'm here?"

"No, I suppose not. I mean, it doesn't come as any smashing surprise *you* are here, but it does rather get to me that anyone at all has come Down Under."

"You thought you worked this alone?"

"There's only one radar station, after all," he said in exasperation.

I had to laugh at that. He and I shared the feeling that Hawk overreacted by sending in the troops like he had. In fact, Hawk had called in all his big guns.

My mind flashed to Elaine Thompson over in New Zealand. Or rather, she'd be there in about a week. I started to mention this to Marian, then bit it back. Paranoia again.

Or simple caution.

If Hawk hadn't told Marian that I, or any other AXE agent, was to assist on this mission, he had a reason.

". . . been a while since I got back from that Malayasia flap," I heard Marian saying. I'd zoned out while he continued to talk. But what he said was inconsequential. He related charming little anecdotes of his rescue mission into Vietnam.

I hate charming little anecdotes.

"Tell me about the radar station," I interrupted. The look on Marian's face turned me colder inside. I'd read his dossier; the man had done good work for AXE. It had to be a slap in the face for him having another agent on "his" assignment. Yet I found myself wondering if Marian hadn't lost his nerve somewhere along the way.

It happens. It worries all of us at one time or another. We have to face incredible danger and respond perfectly. There's never any time to think about the consequences—death—of what we're doing. Afterward, it doesn't pay to dwell on past victories, either. We start to analyze, to criticize, to think that we might have been just a bit luckier than skillful, that it might not happen again. A failure of nerve results if an agent gets too far into such thinking.

Sanford Marian rattled on and on about his past missions and tried to avoid discussing this one. Was this a sign that his best days were past, that he was ready for retirement?

Marian wasn't old enough to have those troubles, I didn't think. He was hardly forty, his sandy hair was a thick bush without a hint of gray, he moved well and, from his last efficiency report, he maintained top scores on marksmanship and physical agility. A lingering aroma hung about the man like a fog. For a few minutes, I failed to recognize it, thinking it nothing more than an effeminate cologne. Then one page of the dossier on the man came back to mind. Marian figured himself to be something of a ladies' man. The miasma he carried was probably his current lady-love's perfume.

"Look," I said. "I didn't want to butt in on your assignment. I was ordered down here." I paused, thinking this through. "If anything, it's a punishment mission for me, playing second fiddle to you."

"Punishment?" His surprise was apparent.

"I didn't do too well on a desert training maneuver," I lied. "I got sloppy. This is something Hawk thought might sharpen my desert skills." Marian's reaction puzzled me even more than ever. He relaxed, yet a wary air hung about his posture. He didn't relax the proper muscles to indicate he believed me. What *had* happened with him?

"Really, old chap, there's not so much to tell on this. Australia's a big continent. Perhaps Hawk feels we can divvy it up and eliminate the problem that much faster."

"It is a big one," I agreed, glad to lighten the mood.

"I've been digging about here in Sydney but haven't come up with a single spot of good information."

"How did the Soviets get the station into Australia?"

"The best I can determine, they landed a submarine. Been extraordinary sub activity off the coast."

"Which coast?"

"All around. Up and down the Great Barrier Reef, over around Perth, some little bit of it near the coast of Tasmania, all around."

"What about New Zealand?"

"Whatever for? That place is dead, as far as military activity goes. No, the Russkies aren't interested in New

Zealand. Their radar station is somewhere on the continent. I fear it's in the Outback."

"The desert?"

My ears shut off the flood of details Marian furnished about the Outback country. My mind was too occupied with this new bit of information. No Russian submarine activity near New Zealand? Was Elaine doomed to sit on the deck of a boat; and do nothing but count penguins? Or was Marian wrong, was the radar station in New Zealand and Elaine got to take it out?

Whatever Hawk's motives for keeping all of us in the dark, it bothered me. I'd spend more time trying to decipher the true reasons from this cryptic morass of conflicting facts than I would finding and destroying the radar station, which on the face of it all, still seemed a trivial assignment.

"The satellite recon over the past several weeks hasn't been able to locate anything. We've even had a few flyovers, clandestine, of course, and drawn naught from those."

"Does the Australian government know anything at all about the Russian station?" I asked.

"Not a bit of it. The fewer people who know of it, the better. That's the word I received."

"Same. It's our mission."

"Yes, old chap, ours."

The word "ours" came out dripping with acid. I can't say I blamed him much. "What do you know of the radar unit itself? Size, power requirements, that sort of thing?"

"The others taken out were conventional C-band radar, range thirty-two thousand miles with a two yard margin of error. I doubt they'd go to the Unified S-band unit. Requires a ten meter dish. The C-band gets by with an aluminium dish, you know."

I smiled at the way he said aluminum. The *aluminium* was so typically British Marian couldn't have been raised anywhere else except within earshot of Bow Bells.

"So this is a smallish unit?"

"And they only operate it intermittently, I'd wager. That makes it deucedly hard to locate. Can't trace back on a radar reflection if they don't run it continually."

"Is there any way we can entice them into longer operation? Some tidbit about a new test at Woomera? Something they'd want badly enough to risk detection?"

"Not a bad idea, but remember, we don't have the Aussies' cooperation. Be a bit dicey releasing the secret and then having one of their blokes find out about it. Could raise nasty questions neither of us would want to answer."

"What progress have you made?"

"Well," said Marian, brushing back his sandy hair and staring into his glass, "not much. I've located a few KGB agents running loose in Sydney. Seems to be more now than even a few weeks ago. That might mean something. Then again, it might not."

I sighed and tried to work this through. More KGB agents didn't signify much of anything, not if Marian had been able to spot them. Australia was an out of the way spot for world espionage, yet it provided an interesting departure point to other parts of the Southern Hemisphere. Entering South America, for instance, was easier from Australia than from either Europe or North America, if you didn't want to answer a lot of questions posed by the authorities. The South American governments tended to be suspicious of anyone to the north of them; Australia escaped their notice, in spite of being part of the British Commonwealth.

Also, Australia provided a good post for commuting to and from the Philippines and Southeast Asia. While the continent had little to offer a spy in terms of usable secrets, it gave a chance to rest before going on to more important locations.

That more KGB agents walked the Sydney streets now than did a couple months ago meant nothing. If anything, it indicated that the Soviets kept their radar station secret from their own people. This wasn't a new development by any means. The Russians often ran several parallel missions, each group ignorant of the existence of any other.

"I think a top-ranking agent might be on his way here," said Marian.

"Who?"

He shrugged. "Can't say for certain. It seems as if our best bet might be to put the snatch on a few of these blokes and ask what's happening."

"I don't like it. That kind of overt activity might tip our hand too soon."

"What hand? I say, old chap, we're in the dark on this. We need a bit of bold action to get us out into the sunlight."

"Make the arrangements," I said. "I'll be in touch with you around ten o'clock tomorrow morning. We can go hunting then."

"Right-o." Marian finished off his whiskey in a single gulp, rose and smoothly pivoted away. His stride was confident, graceful, even elegant. He posed as much an enigma for me as did the radar station

What he suggested wasn't the best course of action, yet it might achieve results. Knowing the Russians as I did, it would be the sheerest luck on our part if we grabbed one of their agents who knew anything about anything. Since Australia provided little more than a stopping off point, R&R, if you will, the KGB agents might not even be on assignment. Any assignment.

Marian was competent. His AXE dossier told me as much. But only one thing counts in this business: current results. Sanford Marian was not delivering and hadn't presented any clear scheme indicating progress in this matter.

I finished my scotch and returned to my room. I was still a few hours short on sleep. After I caught up would be the time to do some hard thinking on all aspects of this assignment.

SEVEN

I felt naked.

Everyone seemed to stare at me, knowing how undressed I was. It was all the result of an overactive imagination, but not having Wilhelmina, Pierre and Hugo with me made me a little paranoid. I hadn't trusted Sanford Marian to accept their shipment, rather, I'd put a package containing my weapons in the diplomatic pouch sent into Canberra every day. From there, one of the embassy staff had shipped my package to Sydney and, if all had gone well, placed it inside a locker at the main train depot.

I didn't have to ask which locker. When I saw one labeled "N3" I knew what was inside. A tiny loop of wire, a quick tug and the locker door opened. Inside was a brown paper wrapped package. Hefting it told me that everything had gone smoothly.

In the men's john, I nestled Pierre in place next to my right thigh, then slipped Wilhelmina into her shoulder holster and Hugo into the sheath on my right forearm. I tensed the muscles once and sent the shining blade rocketing down into my grip. The spring-loaded mechanism worked perfectly.

I felt dressed again. And it was time for me to go to work.

A taxi ride across town took me to a street bordering the Redfern slums. The Soviets didn't keep a very high profile at their way stations. This was definitely the low-rent district. Paint peeled from the house trims; the streets, normally good throughout Sydney, were filled with potholes deep enough to sprain an ankle in. Weeds grew in wild profusion, and here and there were the derelicts of an otherwise pleasant and prosperous society.

"What ho, old chap," came the cheery greeting from the porch of one tumbled-down wood frame house. Sanford Marian sat on the top step, his face dirtied and his clothes disheveled. I felt overdressed, even in a ragged knit shirt and faded jeans, because I wore a jacket to hide Wilhelmina.

"What's been happening?" I asked, sitting beside him.

The man glanced over my clothing and scowled slightly. "The agents are arriving and departing with somewhat more regularity now. I've clocked in five in the past hour. Two have left."

"How many inside?" I studied the house across the street. It had a condemned sign crookedly nailed to the front, just like so many others in this block. Part of urban renewal that hadn't arrived yet, it made a perfect rendezvous point for Russian agents.

In this neighborhood no one asked questions about strange comings and goings.

"I make it out to be a minimum of eight. There's an outside chance the KGB has been augmenting their field force. Might be a few extras. Are you game? Or do you wish to wait until after tea time?"

I snorted. "The Russians don't care about tea or cricket or any of the finer things of civilization."

"Their loss."

I felt a bit like a spectator at a cricket match myself. It had been several days since I'd done anything but travel. The tedium had gotten to me. I wanted action. Now. But rushing into a den of KGB agents wasn't the smartest move in the world, not without doing a little reconnaissance first.

"I'll go look them over."

"Have a set of blueprints with me, if that's what you need," said Marian. He nodded toward a lunch pail setting behind the railing on the porch.

"I'll scout around. Might find some additions that don't show up on the blueprints."

"Ah, yes, alarms and things. I don't believe we have to worry on that score, old chap. The damn Russkies have had budget cutbacks, too. They wouldn't install an expensive alarm system on a throwaway place like this. That house is slated to be torn down in a few months."

I didn't want to argue with Marian. For my taste, this sounded like sloppy thinking on his part. Whether the KGB used this house for a day or a decade, they'd protect it in some way. I intended to find out how before blundering in.

Without another word to Marian, I rose and walked down the block. Turning, lighting a cigarette, I studied my target from all angles. When I'd finished a second cigarette, a good idea of the layout inside had formed, plus some indications of a simple motion-detector alarm system. While the Soviets hadn't gone overboard on spending, they did have a rudimentary electronic surveillance setup.

Getting past it would be simple.

Marian still sat on the porch, as if he didn't have a care in the world. Good cover—or was it stupidity on his part? There didn't seem to be an easy answer to that question. His record hinted at good camouflage; his actions told a different story. Sanford Marian gave every indication of not really caring what the hell he did, or what kind of a mess I got myself into. He looked more and more like an agent who had turned sour.

The sun sank and some of the heat of the summer day vanished. Under the cover of deepening twilight, I started down the alley behind the house. At the back of the house stood large trash bins overflowing with refuse. They provided cover as I worked my way forward. A cleared patch of almost ten feet between my position and the back door leading into the kitchen was protected by a motion sensor.

I dropped to my belly and began inching forward, sticking to shadows, moving so slowly my progress seemed nonexistent. But almost twenty minutes later, my outstretched hand brushed against the foundations of the house. No alarm had warned of my approach.

Still moving slower than molasses on a cold day, I snaked upright and peered into a window into a dining room. Three men and a woman sat at a table playing cards. From the money on the table I guessed at poker. Even the most diligent of KGB agents can be corrupted with Western ways.

I slid along the wall, safer now than I had been out in the open stretch. The motion sensors would be directed outward; I moved under their beam. A second window into the kitchen revealed another pair of agents—a man and a woman. From the way they went at it so hot and heavy, it would take them several minutes to recover if I went in.

So I did.

The man had his pants down—literally—when I walked into the kitchen. He turned. His face contorted into anger, then went slack as I jabbed hard into his solar plexus. He went out like a light. The woman sprawled back on the kitchen table reacted faster than I would have thought possible. Maybe she had been faking her passion.

At any rate, I had to move fast. Hugo pinned her wrist to the wooden table as she reached for a Tokorov 7.655mm automatic.

"*Aiieee*!" she shrieked, as pain flooded her body. There wasn't a second outcry. My knuckles pushed hard into her carotid arteries. In less than a minute she was out cold. I retrieved Hugo and hefted the small Russian automatic. No sense using Wilhelmina's bullets if the KGB supplied ammo for me. I hurried to the door to listen. If the woman's brief outcry had been heard, I might be up to my ears in boiling mad KGB agents.

I strained to hear the conversation going on among the card players in the next room. I almost laughed when I caught the drift of what they were saying. The man I'd knocked out was the local bureau chief and the woman was a new agent—one more intent on getting ahead in KGB ranks than anything else. The card players made crude jokes about how much fun the woman was actually having and how much she was faking.

Glancing back, I made sure both the bureau chief and his mistress were still out cold. Then I moved.

"One word and you're dead," I said quietly to the card players. Four against one is lousy odds, even when the one held an automatic. And the foursome knew it. Even as I told them to stay quiet, I shifted the pistol to my left hand and sent Hugo directly into the windpipe of the man farthest from me.

That reduced my odds, gave the KGB agents something else to think about for a second and permitted me to cross the room. A karate chop to the throat took out the woman. A kick to the groin doubled over one of the two remaining men. And the last man wasn't about to argue now—the Tokorov pointed directly for his head.

"There's no need to shoot," he said softly. Only a slight tremor in his voice betrayed the intense emotion he felt.

"Tie them up. Now. Start with him." I indicated the man groaning and clutching his groin. When that was done, I pointed toward the woman. The third man presented no problem to anyone anymore. He was quite dead. I stripped all of them of their weapons. The pile was large enough for me to open my own pawn shop back in the States. After I'd tied my unwilling helper and gagged all three of the living, I stuffed the spare ammo and clips into my jacket pocket and went off in search of anyone else in the house.

Marian had thought there might be eight. I'd taken six out of the game.

His count was accurate. I decked one man coming out of the john. But the way he thrashed about as he fell overturned a lamp and the table under it. The eighth man came out of a bedroom with guns blazing.

I dodged but still felt a hot crease across my shoulders. Nothing too bad, but enough to let me know how close I'd come to death on my one-man grandstanding play. The KGB agent tried to reach his fallen comrade. I held him back with a few well-placed shots. But this firefight couldn't go on too long. Even in a neighborhood like this, prolonged gunfire would draw police—and crowds.

"Give it up," I called out in Russian. "There are too many of us. We have you!"

He fired with both guns again. Spent brass clattered to the floor like hailstones. I'd never seen anyone fire two guns simultaneously before with such accuracy. Wood splinters threatened to blind me if the bullets causing them didn't ventilate me first. I fired carefully, accurately, and hit the man.

He yelped. The sound told me his wound wasn't serious. I might have done little more than return the scratch he'd already given me.

The firefight had gone on for less than a minute. It stretched like eternity. It'd have to end quickly. I braced myself for a quick frontal assault when I heard a heavy thud from the bedroom where the KGB agent had taken refuge.

"I say, old chap," came a familiar voice, "I do believe there's no need to worry about this bloke any longer. How're you fixed on the others?"

"Marian?" I called, hesitant to believe he'd actually come to my aid. Why, I can't say. This entire sortie had been mine from beginning to end. A good AXE agent should have come in to assist a long time back.

"Right-o."

"That was number eight," I said, still keeping behind the cover of the door frame in the hallway. "The others are already taken out."

"Bravo," he said, emerging from the room. "You do good work, Yank."

"The one in the kitchen is the bureau chief. If he doesn't know anything, no one will."

"All this and identification, too. You are *very* efficient, Carter," Marian said, walking through the dining room as if he were on an afternoon stroll through the British Museum.

"I try," I said dryly.

The bureau chief croaked like a frog as he struggled to regain consciousness. We'd gotten back to him in time. Another few minutes and I would have been caught between the man in the bedroom and the rest of the agents. I pulled the chief into a chair.

"I say, he and this bird . . ." Marian studied the scene for a moment and began to laugh. "And the Soviets are such puritans. I'd always wondered where little Party members came from."

"We've got to make this fast, Marian," I told him. "Do you have the kit?"

"Right here."

He fumbled inside his tattered clothing and withdrew a small kit containing a syringe and a new truth serum the Special Effects Department had come up with. Most of the so-called truth serums work like sodium pentathol to relax and release inhibitions. They aren't actually truth serums in the strictest sense.

This one, still nameless, broke down the mental and physical barriers to truth and actually allowed the questioner to guide the interrogation. It also burned out part of the prefrontal lobes in the victim's brain. It wasn't pleasant, but it worked better than anything else either side had come up with so far.

Sanford Marian injected, I timed. After two minutes, I began asking questions.

"Where is the radar unit located?"

The recitation included a list of every single damned radar station the man had ever seen. I amended the question.

"Where is the Russian radar station in Australia?"

"None," he mumbled, his eyes glassy and rolling up and down.

"Do you know of the stations in India, Japan, the Philippines?"

"No."

"That means," supplied Marian needlessly, "he might not know of the one here."

I glared at him. The sandy-haired agent only smiled and shrugged, as if saying, "That's the way it goes, old chap."

"What is your mission here?"

"To provide a stopover point."

"Anything else?"

"Nothing else. Dead end station. No way out. Punishment. Anastasia!"

"I say, what's he mean by that?" asked Marian.

I pointed to the woman on the table. "That's Anastasia, I suspect. The time's about up on the drug's usefulness. He's starting to free-associate now, and she was on his mind."

"So to speak," said Marian.

"He doesn't know anything. This was a minor station with nothing but agents being shipped to other areas of the world." I hesitated as I looked at the man. He was a KGB bureau chief, my sworn enemy in this mission, yet I felt a pang of regret for what I'd done to him. While the drug wouldn't turn him into a complete vegetable, he'd be much more docile and unable to initiate very much on his own. Someone would have to tell him what to do before he could do it.

Maybe Anastasia would get the power she desired through guiding him.

Maybe it would have been kinder to have put a bullet through his brain. Marian and I left, Anastasia moaning in pain from her cut wrist and bruised neck and the KGB chief babbling on about Leningrad and his wife there.

EIGHT

A dead end. Absolutely. I stared at the maps in front of me on the table and shook my head. Where to start posed more than a simple problem. I cursed Hawk for sending me to Australia, I cursed Marian for not dealing with this problem on his own, and most of all, I cursed myself for being unable to find the single master stroke that would solve the problem and eliminate the radar station.

The information—or lack of it—off the KGB field headquarters hadn't surprised me too much. The Soviets often run several different operations in a single country without telling the local office. This was their equivalent of our "need to know." Still, a bureau chief for the KGB should have heard something. Even if this had been a punishment detail for him screwing up elsewhere, broad hints should have filtered into his office.

For all their bumbling in covert activities, the KGB is usually very efficient at information gathering. And the bureau chief hadn't even heard of the radar stations being placed in the other countries, much less on his home turf.

"Damn!" I cried, slamming my hand down amid the maps. The charts mocked me. So much terrain, such a little radar station. The huge Outback area spread over too much desert for me to ever luck into finding the radar unit. I had to be smart, much smarter than I'd been up to this point. Relying on chance would never drop the unit into my hands.

The names on the map came up familiar and alien at the same time. Alice Springs. Kalgoorlie. Yalata. Woomera.

If I were the Russians' genius who'd thought up this scheme, where would I put the radar unit?

Near a city? No way. Even intermittent operation would be too susceptible to detection. In the harshest portion of the desert? Likewise, no. But for different reasons. There wasn't much water in the Outback, and even radar technicians need to drink occasionally. Hauling the equipment to a remote site didn't seem too plausible, either. A generating unit large enough to run a C-band radar rig is heavy. Supply? They'd need diesel fuel for the generator. Food, water, some replacement of personnel. If they picked a spot too far out in the middle of nowhere, they'd never be seen operating the unit, but they might be picked up ferrying supplies to and fro.

So. No big cities but no desolate reaches either. That left a plethora of small towns like Alice Springs. I doubted anyone would notice the occasional interference from a radar unit in a town where there were more dogs than television sets. Yet I shied away from such an easy answer. Small towns have their own grapevines for gossip. Anyone showing up who hadn't lived there for forty years would be the new kid on the block and open to discussion, just the sort of thing the Russians wouldn't want.

That didn't leave much.

Or did it?

I pored over the maps and located a tiny legend showing where some of the stations were in the Outback. Sheep stations—ranches—dotted the entire countryside. Hundreds, maybe thousands of the stations scattered across the wilderness areas of Australia.

A station operated like a U.S. ranch. Maybe fifty people at the outside actually on it. Supplies had to be carried in from town. No one would think twice about orders from a station owner of some standing. If the Soviets had bought off a station owner, it might not be too hard to keep their presence secret from others working the land.

The idea seemed appealing and plausible. While it hardly pinpointed the radar unit's location, it narrowed the search considerably. If I were right.

I made a mental note to ask Marian about owners with

Russian leanings. Perhaps there were even some Russian immigrants working a station. That might be going too far. The Soviets usually managed to keep a lower profile than that by buying their way into a society. There had to be any number of owners in a financial bind who saw nothing wrong with a measly little radar station planted on the back forty.

The more I thought about it, the more I liked the idea.

I folded my maps and put them away before going out on the small balcony of my hotel room. A second-story view isn't too inspiring, but this hotel wasn't a highrise. I'd wanted a middle-of-the-road location to work from, and it fit nicely. Leaning on the railing, I stared out toward Sydney Harbor.

The topmasts of a cargo ship loomed into view. The clanking sounds of chains came a few minutes later as the ship docked and the unloading began. The salt and sea air made me feel alive, even if those heady odors were intermixed with dead fish and tar.

I took another deep breath and felt the hot crease where the KGB agent's bullet had scored me. As I jerked in response to the momentary pain, a heavy wood spear whirred past my head so close it brushed a few hairs on my scalp. The hard *thunk*! as it buried itself into the wall behind me told the story: If I hadn't moved, I would have been impaled.

Ducking down, I peered through the ornate balcony decoration into the street. A shadow moved away. With a single smooth action, I vaulted the railing and dropped two stories. My knees bent to absorb the impact. Rolling, I came to my feet not ten yards from where my assailant had launched his missile.

"Stop!" I yelled after him. The man's bare feet pounded hard against the pavement. Although I clearly saw the black man didn't wear any shoes, it sounded as if leather struck asphalt.

Wilhelmina came smoothly into my hand, then I stopped. Shooting him on the street would only draw attention. I needed him alive to answer questions. My foray into the KGB office hadn't been too successful. Maybe my would-be assassin could furnish some information.

I holstered my Luger and ran for all I was worth. In less than a block I'd overtaken the man. A last powerful sprint, a dive and down we went in a thrashing, fighting heap. As he turned, my grip slackened in surprise.

All the evidence had been there before me, but I hadn't fully realized before that my assailant was an aborigine. Wild and pagan, he glared at me, then swung a short wooden stick that caught me on the side of the head. Stars spun in crazy circles, but I didn't let loose of his wiry arm.

He hit me again, and this made me mad. I punched, short, hard, quick. My fist buried wrist-deep in his midsection. A loud gust of air from his lungs told me he wasn't going anywhere.

Panting, I stood over him and took a good, long look.

His face had been whitewashed, as had his right hand. He wore a simple breechcloth around his middle. The wooden stick he'd hit me with had been grooved in such a fashion that I decided it had been used as a spear-thrower. With such leverage, even a man of his scrawny build could have heaved a heavy spear the distance up to my balcony.

"Okay," I said, "who are you?"

"Blackfella," was all he said.

He took me unawares, kicking out and hooking his foot behind my knee. I tumbled backward, somersaulted and was on him in an instant. He drew a rusty knife from somewhere, and stabbed.

Blocking the blow with my left forearm, I reacted instinctively. Hugo slipped into my hand, and the point drove in under ribs and up into the man's heart. He died without a sound.

I cleaned the knife and resheathed it, wondering if I should leave the body on the street or if I ought to hide it. My preoccupation had allowed two police squad cars to come up on me from either direction. They had me trapped.

"All right, cobber, don't move!" cried one policeman, a nasty looking revolver aimed directly at me.

I raised my hands, wondering how I was going to explain this.

NINE

"This man seems to have been taken ill," I said, adopting a heavy Germanic accent.

"Ill?" cried one officer. "This abo's stone dead!"

As he turned to look at me, alternatives flashed through my mind, sifted and filtered and left but one choice. Kicking out, I caught him in the side and sent him tumbling over the corpse. The others followed the motion, allowing me to run like hell.

"Stop!" roared the policeman with his gun drawn. I ducked, dodged and darted down an alley. Bits of masonry chipped off as the officer fired. The alley wasn't long, but my chances of reaching the far end before the police rounded the corner and saw me were slim. I saw some garbage cans and dived behind them.

I fingered Wilhelmina, then forgot about using the Luger. I didn't think killing a half dozen policemen constituted an acceptable "expense" for this mission. In other instances, yes, definitely, but locating a radar station that seemed more of an irritant than a major threat to world peace didn't require this kind of wholesale death.

"He's down here, I tell you," declared one policeman. "Hiding behind some of those dust bins."

"He's too fleet of foot. He's out the other end by now," contradicted another.

I crossed my fingers, hoping the one thinking so highly of my speed won out.

He did.

I waited fully a half hour before venturing out. The

streets were clear of police, except for a tight knot around the body of the fallen aborigine. An ambulance whined up even as I stood watching. I walked slowly away from the scene and back to my hotel without further incident. By the time I got out onto my balcony, the ambulance and the body were long gone.

I called up Sanford Marian. I needed information.

"Somebody tried to snuff you, old chap?" he cried in a startled voice.

I wished I could have been present to see his expression, his body language. "Came close," I said. "An aborigine tossed a spear my way using a spear-thrower."

"A *woomera*?"

"What?"

"That's the abo name for spear-thrower. Clever of us to adopt it for our rocket base, don't you think?"

"Yeah, right," I said, trying not to get mad. "What can you tell me about the aborigine?"

"Hard to say, without examining the body. There are quite a few tribes of the beggars in the Outback."

"This one had his face painted white. And his right hand. All he wore was a loincloth."

"Sounds like any number of them, though I'm hardly the expert. In fact, I've never even seen one, not in the flesh. Most Australians living in cities never have. They keep pretty much to the Outback. The abos, that is."

"Is there anything odd in the choice of weapons? He had a rusty knife with him, too."

"No," came the low, drawn-out syllable. "Can't say there is. They are reputedly damned accurate with their spears. The knives used to be chiseled from flint or some other stone until the whitefellas showed up. They got steel knives then."

"Whitefellas?" I asked, remembering the aborigine had called himself "blackfella" when I'd asked who he was.

"They call us that. Any European. Quaint, isn't it?"

I lost my temper then.

"Look, dammit, I nearly got skewered on a Stone Age spear that would have killed me as dead as any twentieth century weapon. I killed a man out there in the street because he was trying to kill me first. I've never even seen an aborigine before, I don't know that many people here in Australia, and I think there's some connection with my mission and this attempt on my life."

"Oh, Nick, don't be so dramatic. How can there be any connection? An ignorant savage knows naught of a radar unit. This is just some bizarre coincidence."

"Why me? Sydney isn't the kind of town where the aborigines run around, painted white and killing off foreigners."

"The abos do manage to stay in their corner of the Outback," Marian conceded.

"He threw the spear and then ran. He tried to kill me, not rob me."

"Don't think they're much on armed robbery, anyway."

"This might be a matter of incredible indifference to you, but I think it's a lead. If I can track down whoever sent that man to kill me, it might lead back to the radar station. The raid on the KGB station alerted the Russians responsible for it, and they tried to eliminate me."

"Farfetched," declared Marian. I pictured him genteelly sniffing into a perfumed handkerchief and dismissing such nonsense entirely. "You ought to drop this matter. Write it off as coincidence."

"Where can I get more information on the aborigines?" My voice carried a steel edge to it that penetrated Marian's cloud of studied insouciance.

"Oh, very well, but I think this is a bloody waste of time. There's a professor at the university who might be able to give you some information on the abos. What's the name . . . oh, yes, Dr. Rhys-Smith. Now, Nick, is there any more I can do?"

"There's nothing more you can do, Marian," I told him coldly.

I slammed down the receiver and steamed at his attitude. While I hardly counted on him to be as concerned for my life as I was, it seemed apparent that the attempt to remove me and the assignment were linked.

I didn't waste any more time. I went to find Rhys-Smith.

TEN

The university campus looked like any other. I found the department of anthropology and asked the secretary for Dr. Rhys-Smith. The look the young woman shot me was one of hatred mixed in with an "of course he wants to see Dr. Rhys-Smith" expression I didn't understand.

"Go on in," the woman said. "Room 2323 down the hall and to the right."

"Thanks," I said. I felt the woman's eyes on me all the way down the corridor.

When I knocked, a muffled voice sang out, "Dammit, come in or do you plan to wait around all day?"

I went in. The tiny cubicle of an office appeared empty until I heard faint rustling noises under the desk. When the owner of the voice surfaced, we both were in for a pleasant surprise.

"You're not that oaf Larry!"

"I was told to meet Dr. Rhys-Smith here," I said.

She brushed back a strand of lustrous brunette hair, "I *am* Dr. Rhys-Smith. Daniela Rhys-Smith. And you are?" As she spoke, she thrust out her hand.

I took it and felt work-hardened calluses, not at all what I'd expected from a professor or such a beautiful woman. "Nick Carter," I said. "I work for Amalgamated Wire and Press Services. I'm here in Australia to do a series of feature articles on the aborigines."

"You've come to the right place. I've managed to establish better rapport with the abos than any woman since Daisy Bates."

"Daisy Bates?"

"A Victorian lady who roamed the Outback for forty-five years. They've named a mountain after her out in Western Australia."

I remembered the name from a map. "Is it so hard for a woman to talk to the aborigines?" I asked.

"Of course it is," she said, a hint of exasperation in her voice. Whoever she was expecting had worked her up into a fine rage. Now that I'd shown up instead, she had to struggle to control it. "The abos consider women fourth-class citizens, not much above their dogs. And sometimes I wonder about that."

"Primitive, aren't they?"

"No more so than most cultures, ours included." She tipped her head sideways and studied me for a moment. "Australian and American. You *are* an American?"

"You hit it on the first shot," I admitted. "Didn't think my accent was so obvious."

"It is," she said without any tact at all. "What can I do for you? In specific? I'm supposed to meet with the department chairman about some positively absurd notion he's taken into his head about cutting back funds."

"It's the same all over," I said. "But what I needed an expert for was a little identification."

"The tribes are all unique in their totems and the way they paint themselves up."

I nodded, then said, "I'm interested in a tribe that white-washes their face and right hand."

For a moment I thought I'd stuck her with a pin instead of asking a simple question. She settled down, one nicely rounded hip perched on the edge of her desk, the long, slender leg swinging back and forth in an unconsciously nervous gesture.

"That's a simple one. Pitjandjara. They also use red ocher on their left hand. Did you notice any there?"

"No, can't say that I did. Pitjandjara, did you say? Where is that tribe located?"

"The map," she said, turning her head and pouting her lips in a peculiar gesture to indicate the far wall. "Central Australia." When she saw my curiosity at the way she pointed, she smiled and explained. "The abos denote direction with that gesture. I picked it up from them."

"How is it that you've been accepted, when other women weren't?"

"I convinced them I'm a witch."

"Are you?" I asked, smiling.

"You better believe it, cobber." Her smile radiated a hundred watts in a fifty-watt world. When the phone rang, she scooped it up and jammed it against her ear. Every movement came with the same ill-suppressed nervous energy. This was one woman who did things rather than sitting around and talking about them.

"I'll go," I said, when I noticed the way her expression changed as she listened. It was like a storm cloud covering the sun. Whatever news she got wasn't good.

"Wait," she said, holding up her hand. She finally slammed down the receiver and muttered, "That ass!"

"I beg your pardon?"

"The goddamn head of this department. He's cut off *all* my research funds into the Pitjandjara manhood rituals. They use a modified form of penis incision along with the ritual circumcision. Damn fool says they've been eating people again, and he doesn't want any professor on his staff to wind up in a cannibal stew."

"The Pitjandjara are cannibals?"

"Of course they are. All the abos are, but it's purely ritual. They do it to increase their *mana,* their store of energy flowing through the world. They aren't indiscriminate about it. No, what that fool really meant was that he'd given *my* money to someone else. Probably that jackass Fontaine over in medieval studies."

She crossed her arms under well-formed breasts and slumped down, her leg swinging even faster now. It didn't take a mind reader to know Daniela Rhys-Smith's entire day had been ruined—maybe her entire year. A thought came to me.

"I think Amalgamated might be able to swing a little extra money, if you'd guide me through the Outback. It would hardly be enough for any full-scale investigation, but you might be able to do some basic work with the Pitjandjara."

"All I'd need would be transportation, food and a few days with the mob."

"Mob?"

"The abos call any family unit a mob. I've got one in particular I'm friendly with. A few hours of interview with Pierce—he's the head man—would be super!"

"This might be dangerous," I said.

"Of course it will," she said, exasperation returning to her voice. "Going into the Outback is *always* dangerous. Snakes, bugs, thirst. But with my budget cut I wouldn't do anything more than sit around here on my thumb for an entire year till next budget. Yes!" she said, jumping to her feet. "I'll be most happy to give you the ten shilling tour of the Outback in exchange for a few hours with the aborigines."

"I'll arrange a plane and see what accomodations can be had."

"I'll need my notebooks, a dozen pens, no make that two, then . . ." Daniela Rhys-Smith was lost in a world of planning what to take.

I reached over and used her phone to call Sanford Marian.

"I say, old chap," came his nasal tones, after I'd explained what I needed, "is this a wise move? Getting a civilian involved? Who is she, after all? I know her by reputation only. This might be a bad breach of security on your part."

"I'll need a light plane," I cut in.

"Oh, very well, but this is a dead end, I'm quite sure. I suppose you'll also need a base of operations. Hmmm, I have a capital notion. I think one of the station owners, Ram Marston, might be amenable to putting you up. He seemed a nice enough bloke the times I met him here in Sydney."

"Where's his station?" I asked. I took Daniela's arm and pulled her over so she could hear Marian's directions. From the way she smiled and nodded, I knew it was perfect. "All right, make the necessary arrangements. We can leave—"

"In the morning," Daniela whispered.

"In the morning," I told Marian.

"Right-o, but this is a waste of time and effort," he finished.

I let him have the last word. I finally felt as if some progress was being made. That it was made in spite of the Australian AXE agent bothered me.

ELEVEN

"It looks like a good way to die," Daniela Rhys-Smith commented, walking slowly around the single engine plane.

I had to admit the airplane had seen better days. The fuselage had been crudely repaired with patches more fitting for a Raggedy Ann doll than an aluminum body; the cramped cockpit had none of the amenities usually associated with flying, such as well-padded seats or very much leg room; and the paint chipped and peeled wherever it had been applied. On the other hand, the engine, for all its wear, ran smoothly, the controls were crisp and the tires looked brand new.

"I've flown worse," I said.

"You're not even going to kick one of the tires?" the woman asked. "That's what amateur pilots always do."

"Maybe when you fly in a better-built plane it's safe to kick tires," I replied, "but if I tried that on this crate, it might fall apart."

"You'd rather it fall apart in midair?"

Daniela joked. Her beautiful face betrayed not one whit of nervousness about this plane or my abilities to fly it. The only outward sign she gave was one of restlessness to be underway. It reminded me of a thoroughbred in the starting gate. Supremely confident of her own abilities, superbly trained, she wanted the race to begin to show off for all the world.

61

After leaving Daniela's office yesterday, I'd gone to the university library and checked her out. Her credentials weren't outstanding, but they offered a hint into her lifestyle, her way of thinking.

She'd been thrown out of three different universities in the late sixties, not for political activity but for failure to get along with her professors. One she'd publicly denounced as a fraud and a bastard. The bastard part was open to conjecture; her charges on the fraud were later substantiated when the man in question had been caught salting an archaeological dig with bone and flint artifacts of his own making. She'd finally graduated from the University of Adelaide near the bottom of her class.

Daniela's career hadn't taken off and run from there, either. Constantly at odds with her superiors, she had been denied tenure once and, if all accounts were remotely true, she'd be denied again in the fall.

She was a firebrand, a rabble-rouser, a woman who thought for herself and devil take the hindmost.

Everything I'd come across also indicated she was one of the leading authorities on the Australian aborigines.

"It doesn't bother you that you've never been up with me in a plane before?" I asked. "I might be lying about being able to fly this refugee from a junk yard."

"It's your life, too," she said, shrugging. "Compared to what we'll face in the Outback, the trip is nothing."

"Climb in. We're going to see if you're right or not."

I did the pre-flight check and found all the instruments responding nicely. The engine revved until it approached red-line, then cooled down a bit and satisfied me. The exterior trappings on the plane weren't awe-inspiring, but the mechanical parts were well-maintained. It was the perfect plane for an AXE agent. Nothing flashy like a new Mitsubishi Diamond U-1, but it'd get us out to Ram Marston's sheep station.

At least Sanford Marian had done something right in arranging that. I'd spoken to him just prior to coming out to the field and he'd again tried to dissuade me.

"I say, old chap," he'd said in that nasal twang of his,

"this is nothing more than a wild goose chase."

"If you have any better ideas, let me hear them."

"The abo had to be a local type. They don't come in from the Outback all that often. I'm checking to see who might have hired him. Some bloke hanging about a pub, no doubt."

"He was a Pitjandjara," I told Marian, "and you're right about one thing. They don't come into the civilized world that often. That's why I want to go to their home territory and find out firsthand what's up. He didn't travel all that way for nothing."

"Bloody waste of time," Marian snorted.

"You follow up where you can. I'll radio back in when I get to Marston's station."

Sanford Marian had hung up on me without even saying goodbye. I took that to mean he was still less than happy to have a second agent on this mission. The powers that be—David Hawk—hadn't made it clear who was in charge and who ran backup. Marian hadn't even been told I was coming, yet Hawk had told me to get in touch with the man as soon as I arrived. Foul-ups in communication like that mean death out in the field.

"Satisfied with the engine?" asked Daniela, trying to find a comfortable spot in her hard seat. I'd already discovered a single spring poking up through the canvas cover on mine. This flight wouldn't be very relaxing, to say the least.

"Let me check out the radio, and we'll be all set to fly." I spun the dials and put on the primitive headphones. The familiar crackle of static cleared up as I contacted the tower requesting permission to take off.

"Destination, PB 11352?" came the inquiry.

I gave it.

"Are·you going to have any dealings with the abos?"

"Yes," I said, wondering what the hell this had to do with flying.

"Please be advised you are to follow strictly all government regulations dealing with the abos."

"Oh, hell," said Daniela, overhearing that part of the speech. She ripped the mike from my hand and almost bellowed, "Who are you to get off telling me where to go and where not to? I'm Professor Rhys-Smith, have studied the abos closely and know more about them than you'll ever know about your very own arse."

"Cleared for takeoff, professor," came the meek reply.

Daniela tossed the mike forward, letting it dangle from its curled cord. She sat back in the seat, mumbling to herself.

"You handled that nicely," I commented. "Are they always like that?"

"Damn bureaucrats," she steamed. "They try to protect the abos from the outer world, then turn around and socialize them to the point of destroying their culture. Can't let in qualified observers, but can send in pinheads who can't do anything but sort papers and destroy one of the few original Stone Age cultures left."

"What have they done? The bureaucrats?" I only half-listened as I taxied the plane out to the assigned runway, then trimmed the flaps and increased engine RPM. By the time the plane was airborne, Daniela had launched into a full-scale discussion of the few merits and many demerits of Australian government policy dealing with the aborigines.

I listened and assimilated what I could. Some of the information might be useful, but most of it dealt with internal policies that were confusing, meaningless, or both. In other words, Australia had a government of rules and regulations like most others in the world.

I leveled off as we flew northwest along the coast. Looking down provided a stunning panorama of coastline. The white waves crashing into the rocky shores produced a steady white aerial display of foam and water droplets intent on refracting the sun's rays. The resulting rainbow twisted and turned under us, even as the nature of the land slowly changed from fertile to barren.

"That's the Nullarbor Plain," she told me. "Runs inland a good ways."

"A real contrast to the area around Sydney."

We flew in silence for another ten minutes, then she asked, "Who are you?"

"I told you. Nick Carter. Reporter for Amalgamated Wire and—"

"And bullshit," she said forcefully. "I've been around reporters a good deal. You make the noises, you sling the lingo, you act the part—and that's the problem. You're acting, not doing."

"Sorry if you feel that way. My boss tells me at times that I'm neither acting nor doing."

"Bullshit to that, too," she said. "I don't like people lying to me. That's what always happens, though."

"That's the attitude that got you fired from one university post and denied tenure once already where you are—and will get you denied again in a few months."

"You pry into strange things for a reporter."

I shrugged. "The first rule is to find out about your sources. You volunteered too easily to go thrashing about in the Outback. I wanted to find out why."

"I told you why."

"And it turned out to be true."

"Are you a copper?" she asked, point-blank.

"Copper?"

"Cop. Flatfoot. Fuzz, Screw. Whatever you Yanks call it these days."

"You're getting too much slang from the movies."

"And I'm not getting any information at all from you. You know more than you told about the Pitjandjara tribesman killed the other day. The police called me in to examine him. No one else knew about the death—or so the police said."

"It happened near my hotel. I was looking out the window."

"'You were looking out the window'," she mocked, "and have good enough eyesight to know that his left hand wasn't painted red."

"I said I didn't notice."

"It wasn't."

"So?"

"I think you were close enough to see that and everything else. I think you killed him."

"If you believe I killed him, why'd you agree to come along with a dangerous felon?"

"There's no other way to get into the Outback. I'm at a critical stage in my research and need to talk with Pierce and some of the other abos."

"For a few hours of talking you're willing to risk possible death?"

"You're not dangerous," she said. Her brown eyes locked with my gray ones. "Leastways, not to me. You're some sort of Yank cop, aren't you?"

"You've been seeing too many movies."

Daniela wouldn't let it rest. She turned in the tiny seat and half-faced me.

"Undercover. Maybe even a top secret spy. An agent for the American government. Is that it?"

"Believe what you like. If I were—and I'm not saying I am—I doubt if I'd be allowed to tell you." If she pushed any further, I didn't know what I'd do with her. My cover was tenuous. Daniela Rhys-Smith could blow everything.

"I won't whisper a word of it. I think it's . . . super!"

This, from her, surprised me no end. The hard-talking, decisive professor of anthropology sounded like a school-girl with a crush on a rock star.

"Tell me about the aborigines," I urged. If Daniela talked about something else, she might forget about delving into my past and my current employment. The ploy worked. I'd touched her start button.

"The abos," she said, launching into a lecture, "are true remnants of the Stone Age." Daniela went on and on. My mind half-listened, my eyes half-watched the terrain and the rest of me worked over the problems ahead. How had the Russians managed to hide a radar unit from the abos? They fared far and wide in their nomadic search for food. They might be primitive but they weren't stupid.

Then something Daniela said triggered my full attention.

"Wait a second. Back up and tell me again about Dreamtime."

"The Dreaming?" she said. "That's one of the least un-derstood parts of the Pitjandjara culture, of any of the abos' cultures. They don't differentiate between this world, what we'd call reality, and their dreams. They think whatever they see in the Dreaming is as real as everything around us."

"So dreams are real and so is the world?"

"Essentially," she said. "It goes even further. I think the Dreaming might be even more important in some ways. All souls, once living and to be living, are to be found there."

"To be living?"

"A woman gives birth. The father is the man who has dreamed that the child is his."

"Makes for interesting disputes," I said.

"Makes for quick death if no man claims the child as his. The tribe kills the baby, just as they kill twins."

"Why's that?"

"Happened in Western culture, too. Remember all the fairy tales about changelings. Good bit of truth in the good-bad dichotomy. But in the Outback, it's more a matter of practicality. A woman can carry only one child—she needs a free arm. It's hard out there. Having both arms occupied with babies removes her from the food-gathering details. People might starve. It's better to kill the twins."

"Both?"

"Naturally. It's a crude method of eugenics."

"Fun people."

"Added fun is that they talk to ghosts as easily as they do 'real people.'"

"How's that?" I asked.

Daniela looked at me strangely. I'd put just a bit too sharp a tone into the question. If this explanation ran like I thought it might, I had my answer about how the Soviets maintained their radar unit in the face of the aborigines' comings and goings.

"The ghosts are those existing in both the Dreaming and the real world. Just because we can't see them doesn't mean they're not there."

"So, and this is just for instance, if a group of Westerners established a small city and convinced the aborigines that they were ghosts, the abos would treat them as if they belonged in another world?"

"That'd be hard to do. The abos are not dumb or wonky."

"Wonky?"

"Crazy." Daniela spun a finger near her temple. "But gaining status as a ghost in the Outback could be a boon. Nothing would be secret from the tribe's shaman. In fact, the shaman might actually seek out the ghosts to confer with them. He's the main interpreter of the Dreaming."

I worked it all over in my mind. A Russian intelligence officer sets himself up as a ghost. He'd be told of all strangers arriving, of the mob's activities and most of all, he'd have the trust of the tribe. Primitive cultures tend to be very private about their ceremonies and life in general. The Pitjandjara weren't any different, I suspected.

"This business about drifting back and forth between Dreamtime and reality intrigues you, doesn't it?" the woman asked. "May I ask why?"

"It all intrigues me. This movement between dreams and the real world interests me more than other items."

"Because someone out there is able to hide. You're a bounty hunter and think someone's hiding among the abos by claiming to be a ghost!"

"You have an active imagination," I said, laughing.

"You are *not* a reporter. Or only a reporter," she amended. "Before we return to Sydney, I'll find out just what you are."

"Now you're starting to sound like a Mata Hari."

"That would have been my best role, if I hadn't become a professor," Daniela said. "Me, the femme fatale. I can see it now. In real life, on the silver screen, even in the dreaming, I'd be . . . Nick, what's wrong?"

The plane lurched violently and almost jerked the wheel from my hands. I fought to control it. When I finally recovered, sweat ran in rivers down my face. Daniela dabbed it off when she saw I wasn't about to abandon my grip for even a second.

"I don't know. It didn't feel like clear air turbulence. I've flown over deserts before. It felt like the engine lost power for a moment."

"Better not land out there. The Nullarbor Plain is deadly during summer. Heat up to a hundred and twenty is ordinary."

"Check the supplies."

"Did before we left," Daniela said. "We've got the usual emergency rations, which means they aren't worth a damn. My supplies, whatever you've got, the spare water, all gives us about a day's worth of bloody rugged walking."

"I wasn't planning on crashing, even this rattle-trap," I said, struggling to smile.

"Good. I don't think we'd last very long. We'd need three or four gallons of water apiece a day in this heat."

"I'm radioing into Yalata to let them know we're having some small problems. Give'em a fix on us, in case."

I hadn't lifted my hand off the wheel for a tenth of a second when the engine lost power again. I grabbed the wheel hard and pulled, to keep us from nose-diving into the desert.

Then the engine exploded.

The wracking shudder that passed through the plane's superstructure told me we'd begin disintegrating before we crashed in the Nullarbor.

TWELVE

The ground rushed up at me through the sheet of flame lunging back from the engine. I fought the controls but made little progress levelling the plane's precipitous descent.

"Chutes!" cried Daniela. "Are there any parachutes?"

"None," I grated between clenched teeth. The wheel pulled back slightly. The muscles bulged on my arms from the strain of getting the wheel back still further. My feet worked the rudders in a furious attempt to keep the plane swinging from side to side so that I might see the terrain through the wall of fire leaping toward me from the engine compartment.

It worked. All of it worked better than we had any right to expect.

The nose pulled up, and we smashed hard into the ground, sending the plane cartwheeling to land upside down.

For a long time I simply hung in the straps, trying to fight off the shock possessing my senses. When I finally realized we'd landed and had survived—so far—another thought lanced through my brain.

"Daniela!" I shouted. "The plane's on fire. We've got to get out. *Now!*"

She moved as if in a dream. The impact had probably given her a slight concussion. No one thinks well after having their brain scrambled around inside the skull. I didn't

70

want to move her, yet had to. I shook her hard enough to get her attention.

"Out! Get out of the plane!"

"Nick, what happened?" Her voice came small, childlike.

I unfastened my seat belt and dropped to the roof. Wiggling around, I managed to get the woman's seat belt undone. I had to kick out one of the windows. The doors had sprung when we landed upside down and were forever sealed. With Daniela cradled in my arms, we crawled through the window and out onto the dry, dusty plains of Nullarbor.

The smell of gasoline leaking from the ruptured fuel lines overpowered me. From the way the engine had exploded in midair, it was pure luck we hadn't gone up in a fireball already. But with the gasoline pouring out of the fuel tanks now, it was only a matter of seconds before everything went up.

"Come on, woman, move!" I shouted. I half-pulled, half-dragged Daniela away from the wreck. She fought me. It might have been the shock of the moment.

"Nick, the supplies. We need the water. The radio! We can call for help!"

The sun beat down fiercely on the top of my head. It wasn't even midday, and I felt as if I were frying. She had a good point about the radio, too.

"Stay here," I told her as I started back for the plane.

The eruption of flame and heat as the plane caught fire lifted me off my feet and casually tossed me aside, refuse no longer wanted. Rolling, I came to my feet swatting out the tiny blazes on the front of my shirt where fiery debris had landed. My eyebrows had been singed and my face had blistered from the explosion. I limped back to Daniela.

"No radio," I said, indicating the intense flames licking about the plane's fuselage.

"No water," she said in a tiny choked voice. "We're dead, Nick, we're *dead*!"

"No we aren't," I said, shaking her hard enough to rattle her teeth. This was hardly the best treatment for someone with a possible concussion, but I needed to get her thinking, to stop her from giving up and dying on the spot.

"No water, we don't know where we are, no hope of rescue. Nick, *no* one knows we're even down. It'll be a long time before the station owner even thinks that we're overdue. We'll be dead by then. No one survives in the desert without water and supplies."

"The aborigines do."

"That's different."

"How?"

"They were raised to this. We weren't."

"How far are we from Yalata? You were the last one to look at the map."

She shrugged and finally said, "Maybe a hundred miles."

"Two days hard walking."

"We'll be dehydrated and out of it before then. The water leaves the body, changes the electrolyte balance and we die."

"We walk at night and stay under shelter in the day," I said. "Maybe we can make some sort of a water trap if we dig down and . . ."

"And put plastic over it," she finished. "I've tried that, Nick. It doesn't work. You can't get more than a teaspoon of water out of this desert. It's *dry*."

I had to admit Daniela had a point. Looking around I saw scant evidence of vegetation, and what I did find all clicked as "poisonous" in my head. In every direction stretched nothing but desert, dry, parched, deadly desert. So much for Hawk's insistence on a desert survival course. Without water, there was no survival.

"What about water holes? There must be some, or the abos wouldn't be able to survive."

"They guard the locations with a religious fervor," Daniela told me. "The watering holes often dry up, too. Especially in summer. Which it is now."

It was January and the middle of summer. I wanted to laugh at the incongruity of it all. If I'd been back in the States, I'd've been on the ski slopes in Aspen. Now I was

Down Under and frying like a piece of bacon on the griddle.

"Yalata's in that direction," said Daniela, pointing directly into the sun. "I don't know how far, not exactly. It might be less than a hundred miles."

I said nothing. I knew it might be more than a hundred, too. Daniela psyched herself up for the trek. Let her keep going, however she had to do it. I wasn't going to rain on her parade.

We walked. I pulled up my shirt to protect the top of my head. In less than ten minutes of walking I found my Luger and Hugo to be gaining weight. After twenty minutes they weighed a ton. When we took a short break after thirty, I felt like Atlas holding up the world, yet I wasn't about to desert my faithful companions. They'd saved me too many times in the past. I relied on them.

We fell into the sparse shade of a stunted tree. The relief I felt was immediate and welcome.

"I don't understand one thing," I managed to mutter between cracked lips. "Where do those hellish bugs come from?" Gnats had been plaguing us the entire way. They didn't sting, they didn't bite, they didn't do anything except cake themselves all over my face, getting into eyes and nostrils and mouth. I choked repeatedly on the insects, whose only purpose in life seemed to make me even more miserable.

"They're just part of the Australian Outback," she said in a voice so low I barely heard her. The heat took a great toll on the woman. I appreciated that. No amount of play-survival prepared me for what I'd already faced.

A hundred miles of desert lay between us and civilization.

"How charming," I said.

The report from Wilhelmina startled both Daniela and me. Something had taken over in my unconscious mind. I reacted before my conscious mind realized it. I'd drawn the Luger and fired, all in one smooth, swift action.

The uncautious rabbit didn't have a chance. It kicked its powerful back legs, then somersaulted forward, the bullet passing through its body and heart.

"Lunch," I said, scrambling out to pick up the carcass. The animal had barely come forth from its burrow. In the hot noonday sun, nothing but Daniela and I stirred. Everything else had its own burrow or nest and wisely stayed there.

I wished we had a burrow.

The thoughts of tularemia and other diseases possibly carried by the rabbit were ignored in favor of drinking the blood and eating the stringy meat. We could have cooked it; we had more than enough dried wood around to fuel a fire. The idea of facing even more heat repelled both of us. And the feel of the raw meat squishing so wetly rejuvenated us, a bit at least.

We rested whenever we found even a tiny bit of shade, which wasn't often. Tramping through the desert got even worse when we ran into some short, sharp-bladed grass. In the American Southwest the barbed, spiked plant would have been Spanish bayonet.

"Spinifex," said Daniela. "Whatever you do, don't step on it. It'll go right through the sole of your shoes."

I found out the hard way. The sharp points had already stripped the leather off the sides of my shoes. A careless step drove one of the spikes up between my toes. It burned like fire, even though I'd not gotten it through my flesh.

We rested while Daniela checked my wound.

"You'll live," she said.

"I certainly hope so."

"Want to get walking again?" she asked wistfully. I knew she hoped for a negative reply.

"I want to get away from the swarms of gnats," I said. "Besides, we can follow the tire track for a while. Keep us away from the spinifex."

"*Tire* tracks?" she asked, her eyes widening. "Where?"

"There," I said, pointing. Deep ruts in the sand looked as if they had been immortalized in stone. I went over to the nearest and kicked. It hurt my foot and didn't disturb the tracks. They were permanent fixtures in the desert. "How'd this happen?" I asked.

"Those might be fifty years old, older. A truck passed by, left its mark, then it rained. The water caused the minerals to rise into the tracks. When the sun dried the land again, the minerals hardened. This is a permanent reminder of an earlier expedition. I've even found cart tracks dating back over a hundred years."

"If this is a truck tread, that means the truck was going somewhere."

"Fifty or more years ago. And," Daniela continued relentlessly smashing hope, "we don't know which direction the truck was going. It might have been going away from Yalata."

"What's the difference? We know what direction we're going. It's actually better if they were leaving Yalata. They'd have driven straight from there."

"You Yanks are always so optimistic," the woman said. "I hope you're right."

"Won't hurt us any more following the tracks, will it?"

She shook her head, turned and began trudging off. I had to admire the way Daniela kept plugging. This was one woman who would never admit even the smallest defeat. She'd fought in the ivory towers of the universities, but her toughness went deeper. Mentally as well as physically she was a scrapper.

We'd survive. Both of us.

It seemed like an eternity in Dante's lowest level of Hell before we came across a dirt road hardly more than the mineralized truck path we followed. But Daniela let loose a whoop that could have been heard halfway back to Sydney.

"Nick, we've done it! This is the Eyre's Highway!"

"This?" I asked skeptically. The dirt road hardly inspired confidence in finding any travellers within the next century.

"It's the major east-west highway through the Nullarbor."

"So?" I said, looking left and right. The horizon stretched further and further—and more and more empty.

"So we walk and soon enough we'll find a cache of water

and food. They're planted every few miles."

I felt like I'd gone five rounds with Death by the time we found one of the caches. I'll admit that the Eyre's Highway doesn't look like much, but the water beside it went down smooth and the rattling, clanky car that we flagged down three hours later looked like the finest chauffeur-driven Rolls Royce Silver Spirit, in spite of being only a battered Ford pickup truck.

In four more hours we were in Yalata, savoring long, cool baths.

THIRTEEN

"You university types must be more careful," the police commissioner pompously told us. "Always getting into some dust-up or another. You might have died out there on the Nullarbor."

"The bloody damned plane crashed," said Daniela. "That wasn't our fault. It crashed and burned. We were damn lucky to get out before it caught fire."

"As I said, you university types never check out your equipment. Many's the time I've rescued some of you from the desert." The man had formed an opinion and that was it. His thoughts were as firmly rutted as the truck tracks we'd found etched like limestone into the hot desert sands.

"And *I'm* a 'university type.' *He's*—"

"I'm from the States," I cut in. "From the University of Southern California."

Daniela shot a look at me indicating she hoped lightning would strike me down on the spot.

"Not satisfied with the home-grown crops of idiots," muttered the commissioner. "Now we have to import them."

"The plane malfunctioned. Fuel line must have ruptured. Could have happened to anyone," I hurried on, to keep Daniela from correcting me. "This matter is hardly a police concern now. We're safe. You didn't have to send out anyone to rescue us."

"True," he mused, sucking on the tip of a walrus mustache. "Where did you say you were headed?"

"Ram Marston's station."

"Can't fly there. No planes available in Yalata at the moment."

"There are other ways," put in Daniela, her voice edged in ice.

"Land Rover, yes," said the commissioner, as if he planned on accompanying us—or renting us the vehicle.

"Capital," I said. Both the commissioner and Daniela glared at me for the slight Britishism. It didn't pay to go only halfway when adopting an accent or mannerisms. All or nothing. I found it harder to pass for a native with the British accent than I did German, Russian or French.

"This station," the commissioner went on. "I'm not familiar with it. Where's it located?"

"A ways south of Amata," furnished Daniela. "Just at the edge of the Victorian Desert."

"Where the Desert meets the Nullarbor. Rough country, that."

I studied a map hung on the commissioner's wall while Daniela and he talked. I was confident now that she'd either realized I wanted to be known as another academic, or she'd forgotten it in her rush to comment on other things. I found Yalata, traced a route directly east to Woomera, then completed the equilateral triangle up to Coober Pedy and up a bit further north to Amata. Ram Marston's station lay near enough strategic sites to make it of interest to the Russians for a radar site.

He was within easy monitoring distance of Woomera. He might even be able to see launches visually. And there was something else still nagging at the back of my mind, something which might slander a fellow AXE agent: Sanford Marian had suggested Marston's station as a base of operation.

"Do you think we'll have any trouble renting a jeep?" I asked.

"Not hardly, not this time of season," the commissioner said. "Only damn fools go out driving in summer."

"Well," I said, cutting off Daniela's nasty reply, "these

damn fools would appreciate a name and location for renting a four-wheel drive.''

After we left with the information, Daniela jabbed me hard in the ribs. I winced.

"Why'd you do that?"

"You deserve it, you bloody Yank. Why'd you take that lip off the commissioner?"

"I didn't see anything to be gained by antagonizing him. You were pushing him so far he was ready to throw us in jail."

"For what? *We* haven't done anything." She was working herself up into a fine rage.

"Save your energy," I told Daniela. "Driving isn't as easy as flying, and there's a lot of the Nullarbor Plains between us and—"

"And the Victorian Desert," she finished for me. I wished there was some way of curing her of the habit of finishing my sentences.

The woman stared at me for a moment, her dark eyes wide and innocent. "You're really quite a man, aren't you?" she said, surprising me. This compliment was the last thing I expected her to utter.

"Thanks, I guess," I said. "I do my job. That's all that can be asked of anyone."

"Ah, the *job*. Now it's university researcher. UCLA, was it?"

"USC," I corrected. "I always keep my stories straight. It helps me out of a lot of jams."

She laughed and turned away. She was a complex woman. I didn't think she would betray my identity—or my cover—to the commissioner. Daniela enjoyed the intrigue. To her it was nothing more than a game.

To me it was life and death.

"I feel as if my body is rejecting me," I moaned. "My kidneys have been pounded into bloody pulps."

"Good," Daniela said crisply. "We can have them for supper."

We'd been driving hard all day long. The Eyre's Highway wasn't any more than a dirt path, and I'd gladly turned north off it heading for Amata. I hadn't counted on the road we'd taken to be even worse. It consisted of nothing more than parallel bumps. I'd started to drive off on the "shoulder" of the road but Daniela had stopped me.

The spinifex had adapted itself nicely to destroying tires. I kept on the bumpy road, going slowly until I discovered a bone-rattling trick. The vibration and pain resulting from going over the bumps at sixty miles an hour wasn't any worse than at ten. In fact, I felt the Land Rover responding better at the higher speed. Its shock absorbers didn't have time to spring around when I drove fast; there might have been another explanation like becoming airborne and only touching every third rut, but I didn't want to hear it.

I just wanted a warm bath to soothe my aching muscles.

Just as I started to feel my shoulders begin to knot and tense, Daniela's strong hands moved along the ridges of muscle, massaging, kneading, turning the tenseness back into usable muscle.

"Thanks," I said. Again she'd done the unexpected. Daniela Rhys-Smith was so wrapped up in her research and herself that I hadn't thought she'd notice anything outside of her tiny world.

"Feel better?" she asked.

"Much. I'd be even better off if there was some way of avoiding the dust cloud." Glancing in the rear view mirror showed only a curtain of brown behind us. Ahead wasn't much better, though we did stir up a good deal of the storm by simply rocketing down the road.

"The winds will die down near sunset," she assured me. "That's when the aborigines begin their religious ceremonies. I do so hope we can arrive at this bloke Marston's station by noon tomorrow. I want to get everything ready for the evening ceremonies tomorrow night."

"How do you know Marston has any abos working his station?" I asked.

"The Pitjandjara are moving through this entire area. There has to be some group of them near Marston's. He has water; they need it. Right?"

It had become ingrained in my skull that water dominated life in the Outback. Few holes contained more than a cupful and those were jealously guarded tribal secrets. It meant the difference between survival and death in the hot sun. Of course there would be aborigines at Marston's place, if there were any abos at all in the vicinity.

"I'm trying to get a better line on their rituals involving the *tjurunga*. These are their most sacred relics." She laughed. "I remember one researcher who made a friend for life. One of the men in a tribe dropped a stone totem and broke it. That's an automatic death penalty."

"What happened?"

"The anthropologist used epoxy to glue the stone back together. No one else ever know. Did he ever get a wealth of information about their rituals! The abo fell all over himself telling his tribe's most cherished secrets."

"What about the totems? I don't understand how they use them."

"Each tribe has a totem animal. A kangaroo, a wombat, a bird. They feel their spirit is enhanced if they eat their totem. A very solemn and rare ceremony. I'm hoping to get good pictures of it. I have a camera with infrared film in it."

"Where'd you get that?" I asked. "Your stuff was lost in the plane crash."

"Bought it in Yalata. On university credit." She smiled wickedly. "My head will be used in the next cricket match, I'm sure, because I don't have credit privileges with the university comptroller." Daniela broke out laughing at her coup.

I wished I'd had more of a chance to restock my own personal supplies in Yalata, but arranging for this Land Rover had taken too much time. Still, I had the supplies I really needed. Wilhelmina hung in her shoulder holster, in spite of the heat and dust. Hugo rested in his sheath. My tiny gas bomb Pierre rubbed against the inside of my right thigh. Those were the supplies I needed—those and brains.

In spite of the crash, in spite of the hike through the deadly desert, in spite of everything, I felt more alive now than I had since beginning this assignment. I was out *doing* something. Sanford Marian could pursue his clues back in Sydney. Here, I felt I was accomplishing something. That might be an illusion, but action always counts more than simple planning. You can plan for a lifetime and do nothing.

I did. I succeeded.

"Let's make camp here for the night," I said. "The twilight's too tricky to drive in, and the headlights won't give us much light on the road."

"Damn dust does obscure the headlamps," she agreed. "There's a likely looking spot. With luck, we can dine like the abos."

"On ants and boiled roots," I said without much enthusiasm.

"Maybe I can open a can of beans instead."

"Thanks, I'd prefer it."

"Oh, you Yanks and your tender stomachs." Daniela piled out of the truck and began fussing about making a fire. While she tended to the food, I checked out the truck, fixed a few nuts and bolts that had jarred loose and finally gave the four-wheeler a clean bill of health. The truck had been built for rough use, and today it got more than its share.

"Supper about ready?" I asked, wiping the grease off my hands.

"As soon as the billy boils." She nudged a blackened quart can on the fire.

"What's that?" I asked.

"Tea."

"Why call it a billy?"

"That's the can. The French brought in canned beef— *boeuf bouilli*—in the early days. In Australia, every foreign phrase gets bastardized fast. So, today we boil our tea in a billy can."

"Logical," I said. But I didn't want history, I wanted rest. The food was simple, the tea good and the surroundings unearthly. We'd camped near a small stand of trees. For a long while I couldn't figure out what made this so restful, so pleasant. Then I realized these were sandalwood trees. A million cones of sandalwood incense were burned in the U.S. each year and none approached the heavenly fragrance given off naturally by these trees.

"Nice, isn't it?" asked Daniela, sliding down beside me on the blanket I'd stretched out.

"Not even the ants seem inclined to bother us tonight."

I stared at the stars overhead, at the strange constellations, the broken configuration that was the Southern Cross. This might have been an alien world light years away circling another sun.

I felt Daniela's hand resting on mine.

I turned my head and our gazes locked. The way I felt in that moment was different than I've ever felt before. Cut off from civilization, we were the only humans in the known universe. She bent down, and I kissed her full on the lips.

Our bodies crushed together under the strange stars above. I tasted the wine of her lips even as I inhaled and took in a lungful of sandalwood and the subtle perfume of a woman aroused.

"Oh, Nick, make love to me," she said. I didn't need any real urging. My fingers worked slowly down the front of her shirt, unbuttoning it and then immediately kissing the newly exposed flesh. Daniela trembled a little from the cold by the time I stripped off her shirt and left her naked to the waist. Her breasts crinkled with gooseflesh. I kissed the cold away.

We struggled passionately, undressing each other further. By the time we were ready for the next scene in our passion play, I'd pulled the blanket up to cover us. My hands touched rough wool and satiny flesh. As I moved my fingers up, I discovered she was ready for me.

"Hurry," she moaned softly.

I didn't hurry. Every move was deliberate, slow, precise. Our passions mounted to the point where neither of us could hold back any longer—and still I hung in there. Daniela thrashed about under me, but still I kept on, relentlessly giving her more and more pleasure.

When I could no longer stand the tension in my own loins, I gasped, lunged and lay locked in her arms afterward. Cool fingers of breeze caressed my naked back while her warmer ones worked lower.

"Who are you, Nick?" she finally asked, her eyes bright in the light from the campfire.

"I'm whoever you want me to be. A reporter, a movie star, a spy, a professor from USC, anyone you want."

"You're my very own spy," she said softly, burying her face in my shoulder. I felt her warm breath slow and become more regular until she fell fast asleep. Rolling off her, I kept my arms around her warm, lush body. She fantasized me as a spy. I doubted she would ever reveal such a wild notion in public, but still I wondered what she really thought about me. Coming into her office and life, offering her a brief shot at finishing her research, who did she think I really was?

It didn't matter. All that mattered was my mission. And right now, under the stars and sandalwood tree, I felt the conclusion within my grasp. Power flowed into me and assured me of my invincibility.

FOURTEEN

"How can we have gotten lost?" I demanded. "There's nothing to get us off the track. And you said there were only about six tracks into aborigine territory." I was mad, more at myself than at Daniela. Somewhere I'd made a wrong decision, and we hadn't ended up in Marston's station by noon. It was well past three, and we had no idea where we were.

"It happens," she said with equanimity. "The Outback doesn't have convenient signposts like Manhattan."

"What would you know about Manhattan?"

"More than *you* know about the Outback, that's for certain," she said.

I remembered seeing one sign: Last Reliable Water Supply for 500 Miles. That didn't inspire confidence, although this time we weren't marooned in the desert without water. Two large tanks slurshed and gurgled in the back of the truck. We had enough water to last another week, maybe longer.

The desert stretched uniformly in all directions. At the very limits of vision hovered mountains, tall ones. To the south rose Mt. Harriet, to the west Mt. Davies in the Tomkinson Range, the Musgraves ran to the east and northeast, while the Mann Range circled around to the north. And every single square inch of land between all those mountains was desert.

"I followed the map. See," I said, my finger stabbing

down to indicate where we'd been. "We left camp and drove due north. And now we're going straight into the setting sun, almost due west."

"The road wasn't the one we wanted."

What to do now preyed on my mind. There wasn't any point in going ahead since we didn't have a destination. We wanted a spot to the north. I actually thought about cutting across country and braving the dangers of the tire-piercing spinifex, then discarded that as a bad idea. We'd have to keep to an already pioneered trail if we didn't want to ruin our tires and be afoot again.

"Turn back?" I asked. I was loath to do this. It was tantamount to admitting defeat.

"No!" she snapped. I knew then that this trip meant as much to Daniela as it did to me, but for different reasons. She might be restricted to the campus after we returned. Certainly, all her research funds would be cut off. This presented a golden opportunity for her to finish off an anthropological coup.

I was sure that, had she known of my mission, she would have still put hers ahead in priority. Academics tended to see the world in very limited terms.

"We can't go wandering off. There has to be some way to figure out where to go."

I really knew where we were. It had to be hell. The heat actually blistered the paint on the hood, and sweat ran in continuous rivers down my body, in spite of the fact that the truck roof shielded us from the deadly sun. Inside the temperature ran over a hundred. Outside, I could only guess—perhaps as much as one hundred and twenty.

"If we keep going for another few hours, we might be able to make heads or tails out of this," she said. "Then, if we can't, *then* we turn back."

It sounded like good advice to me. I drove on, into the sunset although that had to be at right angles to the direction I wanted to go. I kept looking for a likely spot to cut off the path and turn north. The spinifex grew more and more abundantly, as if to spite me. The truck's tires wouldn't survive ten feet of that incredibly tough, sharp plant.

"Nick," she said softly. At first, I thought I hallucinated. Daniela never spoke so quietly. When she repeated it, I turned. Her eyes were moist with unshed tears.

"What's wrong?" I asked, concerned.

"About last night. I . . . I normally don't do bloody foolish things like that."

"Maybe you ought to indulge more often."

"Oh, you," she said, smiling. "I meant I don't find many men like you."

"If this is supposed to be a compliment, keep going."

"The men around the university are so . . . different. Poofs, many of them. And the ones that aren't are full of themselves. You are so in control of yourself, so much a man and yet you don't go around flaunting it."

"I don't feel very manly right now. I think we're still lost. I've been driving for hours and haven't seen a sign of a cut-off going north. We're sixty miles to the west of where we want to be."

"And it's getting dark," she said needlessly.

While I knew there weren't any large animals in the Outback, I had to think a bit about the packs of wild dogs running free. A pack of dingoes might be worse than a lion on the African veldt.

"Let's stop and camp."

"Keep driving, for another few minutes. I *feel* as if something's going to happen."

"I'm not one to dispute woman's intuition."

I didn't tell Daniela that I had the same feeling. A sixth sense develops when you live life on the edge as I do. That feeling either works and keeps you alive or it fails and you die. I'm still living, so I trust it whenever possible. This seemed like an innocuous time to trust my instincts.

"Ahead!" Daniela shouted fifteen minutes later.

Lined in the headlights stood a solemn, barbaric figure. His face glowed white and his left hand had alternating red and white stripes painted on it. Only a simple loincloth covered his middle. In one hand he held a spear and woomera. The other hand hung limp at his side.

I braked and sent a cloud of dust rising to obscure the

scene. When the cloud settled again I half expected to see the ghostly figure gone. He still stood in the middle of the road.

"Let me talk with him," exclaimed Daniela, already leaving the truck cab. I followed her closely. I remembered how deadly accurate the aborigine back in Sydney had been with his spear.

The abo grunted and gestured. Daniela turned to me and said in an aside, "He asked where we're going."

"So answer him. Get directions. He must be the equivalent of an Outback traffic cop."

She smiled.

"*Yaal wanning*?" she said. "*Teiwa teiwa njina.*"

The abo nodded and pointed, in the same manner Daniela had when I'd first met her. The aborigine pursed his lips and lifted his chin.

"I told him we were going to a camp a long way off. He recognized the place immediately."

"*Ma pitja!*" the aborigine cried suddenly.

Daniela stiffened. "He just told us to get the hell out of here. I'll have to do some fancy talking. Explain who I am. He doesn't want to talk with a woman; he doesn't know me by reputation."

"Let me give it a try, then," I said.

"Nick, this can be dangerous." She laid a hand on my arm. She trembled slightly.

"Hey there," I said loudly. "Who are you?"

"Blackfella," he answered promptly.

"This whitefella—me—needs directions from my goodfriend—you."

"You plenny friend?" he asked suspiciously.

"I'm Nick. Who are you?"

"Mickey."

"Hey, our names are similar. Do you suppose we're related?"

I spent the next five minutes embarked on the weirdest genealogical tracing ever done, proving that Mickey and I were distant relatives through an ancestor of his who had come to Australia from Dublin, Ireland. By the time we'd finished with this, we were on good terms.

"You did the right thing, Nick," said Daniela quietly. "He would have killed you if you hadn't established some sort of familial relationship."

"How nice of you to tell me now," I said.

"Pitjandjara, blackfella Pitjandjara," Mickey said suddenly.

I raised my eyebrows, and Daniela smiled broadly, saying to me, "This is our lucky day. He's a member of the tribe I'm seeking. Get him to take us to Pierce."

"Pierce?" asked the abo. "Pierce bigfella leader."

"We know Pierce. We're good friends," Daniela said.

The aborigine nodded and rose, starting off into the night.

"What now?" I asked, watching the receding figure.

"We follow. There's not much else we can do."

I heaved a sigh and cast a fond look back at the truck. It was a fortress in this wilderness, and I had to abandon it to follow a Stone Age savage into the desert.

I had to run to catch up with Daniela and Mickey.

FIFTEEN

"Aieeee!" came the blood-curdling shriek. Wilhelmina came instantly into my hand. Daniela restrained me as the aborigines shouted and circled us. I saw the problem. There wasn't any way I could possibly take out any significant number of them before they killed the pair of us. I relaxed a little, putting the Luger back into its sweat-soaked holster. I'd have to let Daniela talk us out of this.

"It's fine, Nick," she said, an eagerness in her voice. "This is the mob I sought. That one's Pierce, their chief."

Pierce didn't look much different from any of the other men. He didn't have any outward insignia showing his exalted status. In fact, he was a little shorter than the others, barely topping five feet. But the thick, almost-white blond hair set him apart from the others. While they had light hair, it didn't have the same curly, almost Scandinavian quality to it.

"Debbil Daniela," Pierce said, stepping forward. "You were in city."

"I've come back to talk with my friends, to share your magic, to sample the power of your totem." This pleased the aborigine. He nodded solemnly and didn't use his knife on her. "I come with another friend, a man related to Mickey." She indicated the abo who had found us. Daniela slipped into the natives' language to further indicate the strength of the familial ties between Mickey and me.

I didn't know whether to be flattered or laugh myself sick.

Finally, Daniela turned back to me and said, "This is

better than I'd hoped. They are gathering for a *corroboree.*"

"Proper big business *corroboree*," said Pierce.

"That's a religious ceremony. This is *perfect* for what I need, Nick!" The woman looked more radiant than I'd ever seen her. Daniela Rhys-Smith was again in her milieu.

"Is it rare?" I asked.

"Very."

"Ask why they're holding it now."

"Nick! I *can't*!" she protested. "That would violate their sense of priorities. Whatever happens, we don't want to upset them. Their religion is all they have. It means everything to them. It orders their lives, gives them guidelines for behavior, puts them into contact with the Dreamtime."

"And ghosts?" I asked.

"Ghosts!" exclaimed Pierce. "Many ghosts pass by, plenny time lately."

"How's that?" I'd forgotten the man stood so close while I talked with Daniela. A mistake. These were Stone Age savages, true, but they were also highly adapted to their environment. Because they painted themselves white and red and wore loincloths, when they wore anything at all, didn't mean they were deaf or didn't understand English.

"Many ghosts lately," repeated Pierce. The small aborigine made a grand gesture encompassing all of the Outback. "More than ever I seen in my life."

"Tell me about them," I urged.

Daniela elbowed me in the ribs. This might violate their religious tenets, but I had to find out. A radar station couldn't be hidden from the abos; it had to be explained away. The best way of doing that was to tie it in with their idea of Dreamtime. If the Russians convinced Pierce and his shaman that the radar unit and its technicians were all "proper Dreamfellas" the aborigines wouldn't even mention it outside their small tribe.

Perfect cover.

The man shrugged, as if it meant little. "Lots more ghosts," was all he said.

"When? Since when have their been more ghosts?"

"Nick," said Daniela uneasily. "Don't press the issue with him. Pierce is more understanding about whitefella ways than most, but if you don't couch the questions in the right manner, he can get bloody nasty about it. And you're coming close to the limit."

I didn't see any change in the man's expression, but I took Daniela's word for it. In a way, I had a bit of information I hadn't had before. There was some strange activity going on in this vicinity. By the time we got to Marston's station, I might have enough data to make a decision on what to do next.

If luck ran with me and the radar station was nearby, the next move on my part would be to destroy it and the technicians running it.

"When is the *corroboree*?" I asked, changing the subject.

"Tomorrow night. Tonight is a gathering, a feast, with the main ceremonies tomorrow."

"I could do with a little food," I said, trying to remember the last meal I'd had. When I did, I shuddered a little. Daniela prepared the food as well as anyone could, but it had still been canned.

"They've got all the tucker set out," the woman said, pointing. I noticed the fire with several billys boiling in it. The fragrance of roasting meat penetrated through the heavier odors of firewood and boiled tea.

"Not human, I trust."

Daniela laughed and shook her head. A strand of hair came loose and fell across her forehead. The lustrous gleam to that brunette cascade brought back the memory of how we'd spent the prior night.

"Nothing so elaborate," she said. "Pierce downed a kangaroo this afternoon. We're having red 'roo for dinner."

I sampled everything, hoping this was the polite way of responding. Most of the food was simple, boiled leaves, honey ants, the cooked kangaroo steak. I washed it all down with plenty of the bitter black tea.

Immediately after eating, the entire camp prepared for sleep. I took the opportunity to slip out of camp to do a little recon work. From Pierce I'd gotten a pretty good idea where Marston's station lay. Less than two hours drive to the north, the main house on the station seemed ideal for all sorts of clandestine activity.

Anywhere in this barren desert did, for that matter.

I skirted the edge of a large dune, prowling about hoping to catch sight of one of Pierce's ghosts. Instead, two abo guards sighted me. The first hint I had of being spotted was the hiss of a spear in mid-flight. I weaved and fell face-forward into the sand.

The spear missed me by a fraction of an inch.

Twisting over the top of the dune, I rolled down the other side and tried to figure out what to do. I wasn't about to let them catch me; their initial response had been to kill. I doubted talking it over with Pierce's guards would result in much more than a second spear, one aimed more accurately for my belly.

The pair came over the top of the dune, not even bothering to hide their silhouettes against the nighttime sky. The moon wasn't up yet but, the illumination from the southern constellations provided the contrast. It was an easy shot with my Luger. I held back. Killing them didn't solve any of my problems.

I ran down a rocky ravine, jumped onto the bank and doubled back. I passed both men as they followed my trail. When they'd stalked by my hidden position on the bank, I jumped. A hard fist to the temple knocked one out instantly. The other moved faster than I would have thought possible. A long-bladed knife slashed through the air between us, holding me at bay.

Kicking out, I sent the knife sailing. I spun, used a roundabout kick to the man's midsection and then finished him off with a short punch to the side of his neck. I missed as he fell; his shortness threw off my aim. Knuckles grated against jawbone. I winced and rubbed my injured hand.

The two aborigines sprawled on the rocky floor of the ravine. My recon mission had been a flop. I returned to camp and slipped between dirty blankets. With thoughts of ghosts drifting through my Dreamings, I passed a restless night.

SIXTEEN

I awoke to the sound of a loud argument. I tried not to be too blatant about it as I pulled Wilhelmina out under my blanket and opened my eyes. Daniela and Pierce stood less than ten feet away, shouting at each other. The language they used would have blistered the ears of a veteran long-shoreman, yet neither seemed angry.

"Stupid bloody bitch give *all* blackfellas ride," insisted Pierce.

"Like bloody hell, we will!" raged Daniela. I hardly recognized this woman as the same one back in a Sydney university. She glowed with an inner light now that told she had found her place in the world. She cared for these people, cared for them in a way I'd never fully understand. She belonged with them, as much as she belonged in a class-room teaching others about aborigine culture.

"What's wrong?" I asked. My pistol slipped back into hiding. There wasn't any real danger I saw, just argument for the sake of argument.

"This bloody fool wants us to take his entire tribe to Marston's station. The Land Rover won't hold that many."

"For plenny big proper *corroboree* we need all Pitjand-jara blackfellas."

"That's only about fifteen or so," I pointed out. "Unless he's talking about taking the women and children, too." Looking around, I wondered how the women ever survived. They were truly second-class citizens in this culture.

94

The children, on the other hand, both male and female, seemed to occupy a strange niche. No adult ever corrected a child, no matter what was done. It was almost as if the children were ghosts flitting through an adult world, beneath notice, beneath contempt.

"Pierce means *all* the tribe. The whole bloody mob of them. No!"

I let Daniela carry through with the arguing. While the Rover might take the fifteen men, with a considerable amount of crowding and all of them standing in the back, there wasn't any way we could handle over forty people.

"Pierce doesn't understand about numbers, Nick," Daniela finally said to me when the argument had cooled down. "His tribe's one of the more advanced. They can handle the concept of four."

"Four?"

"One, two," she said, "then, one, two again. That's it."

"Not even five, like five fingers on one hand?" It seemed incredible to me.

"He really doesn't know how many people he has in his tribe, except that he knows them by name and relationship with the others."

"This place is a census taker's nightmare," I muttered.

"It's a nightmare in many other ways," she said. Then her smile brightened the mood as she added, "It's also a paradise for people like me. I enjoy poking about in odd nooks and crannies getting every single datum from them."

"You should be a detective, not an anthropologist."

"There's a difference?" she asked.

"Okay," I said, changing the subject to keep her mind from working on exactly who I was and what I did out here, "When do we leave? I assume you've worked out the details concerning Pierce and how many of his friends he takes along."

"All the men will go with us. Fifteen of them. The women and children will follow, since they don't take part in this particular ceremony."

"Do the women take part in *any* of the ceremonies?" I asked.

Daniela seemed shocked at the question.

"Of course they bloody well do! They have *many* ceremonies of their own. This particular one has to do with
manhood. One of Pierce's sons is to be initiated into the
tribe, into manhood. Ritual circumcision." The gusto
Daniela took in discussing this made me wonder about her
motives.

"As long as Pierce knows the way to Marston's sheep
station, I'll gladly take along as many as I can squeeze into
the truck," I said. "He does know the way?"

"Yes," she said, drawing out the word. "This is something I must look into one day. The abos always seem to
know exactly where they are in the Outback, yet they don't
have compasses or maps. They carry an incredible amount
of information around in their heads. Imagine, Nick, each
shaman knows *all* the lore of his tribe, of his culture. All!"

I remembered someone telling me the last man in Western culture who could make that claim—and maybe not lie
too much—was Albertus Magnus in the twelfth century.
And they'd made him a saint. This only provided another
indication of the huge separation in cultures between the
Pitjandjara and the nosy, inquisitive "whitefellas."

We trooped back to the truck, the men climbed aboard,
hanging onto every single protuberance they could find,
Pierce almost sitting in my lap in the cab. I would have
preferred Daniela there, but the native chief took such
childlike delight in his post, I didn't have the heart to tell
him to move.

"Hurry, hurry!" he cried.

I rattled off in the direction he indicated. In only a few
minutes I realized it wouldn't be possible for me to go too
fast for these men. They loved the sensation of riding in a
truck, of moving without having to use their own feet. I
gave them a real thrill, speeding along the rough desert,
swerving to avoid patches of spinifex, bouncing so hard I
was sure the headache would never go away.

And all the while they whooped and cheered me on. I
might not know all there was to know about my culture, but
Pierce seemed inclined to want to canonize me for the ex-
citing trip.

"Get off here," he said suddenly. I braked and the men poured off the truck like water from a roof in a rainstorm. "Ram Marston place not far." And that was it. Pierce and his men stalked off among the rocky upjuttings in the desert floor, heading for their ceremonial grounds.

"We've been invited tonight, Nick," said Daniela, heaving a sigh of relief. "If you don't kill us with your wild driving."

"Let's get to Marston's," I said. "I think I need a little relaxing of my own."

SEVENTEEN

"This must be the place," I said.

"You sound skeptical," answered Daniela.

"This is a pretty barren territory. Nothing but desert. I'd expected more, like fields with lush, green grass for the sheep to graze, things like that."

She laughed and shook her head.

"It's not that way in Australia, Nick. Not in the Outback, at any rate. Marston is probably a fabulously wealthy man owning millions of acres of land. Or at least hundreds of thousands."

"The land can't be worth anything," I protested. "It's desert."

"Anyone can be rich, if he owns enough of something, even if it's worthless."

I thought about that. I wouldn't give a penny a section for this land, but that still made Marston rich enough. As we drove in I noticed a small airfield with a pair of single engine planes parked near a wooden shed. Several four-wheel vehicles were in various stages of repair or scavenging near the main house, and the sight of an old-fashioned barn made me think of dozens of Hollywood westerns I'd ever seen. It was the kind of structure all the settlers came from miles around to help raise. The image was so strong I almost heard the fiddle playing, the caller bellowing out his square dance routines and smelled the hay in the field.

But the field was a rocky expanse filled with spinifex. At best, sheep found the grazing tough around the house and barn. At worst, Marston had to bring in feed for them.

I pulled up beside a Land Rover that might have been the clone of the one I drove. Daniela and I got out, thankful for the chance to stretch tired muscles. We'd only been on the road for a couple of hours, but it was a rough road and having all of Pierce's tribe along for the ride hadn't improved my disposition. The only positive factor in allowing the aborigines to hitch a ride with us was their ability to guide us through the desert with uncanny accuracy. Pierce had saved us from having to retrace our steps and venturing into barely explored territory with little more than hope and a bad map.

I swatted at my clothing and produced a dust cloud of choking proportions. Even in the truck cab I'd been thoroughly dusted. While the gnats didn't seem as bad here as they had in the Nullarbor, they presented a continual reminder to keep my mouth shut and my eyes squinted.

"Ho there," came a deep bass voice booming from the interior of the house. "Who might you be?"

"Daniela Rhys-Smith," spoke up the woman without a second's hesitation. "And this is a reporter, Nick Carter."

I decided she'd done the right thing introducing me as a reporter. This was probably the cover Sanford Marian had mentioned when talking with Marston. The researcher from USC cover had been a later improvisation. If anyone tracked back along where I'd been in Australia, they wouldn't have a difficult time finding contradictory stories. I'd have to finish off the assignment before anyone serious enough about proving my identity tried that.

"Rhys-Smith? Carter?" came the incredulous voice. "But you . . . you're . . ."

"We arrived a little late. Sorry about that, Mr. Marston," I said. I wondered at his incredulity.

"But your plane. I mean you were supposed to arrive by plane."

I took a good look at the man. He still stood in the shade of the large overhanging roof but the bright sunlight provided enough light for me to catch all but the minor contours of his face. Big, burly, the man looked like the pioneer type enjoying living—and fighting—in the Australian Outback. Whaleboned, sandy-haired, he stood slightly bowlegged with his arms hanging at his sides. This made him appear more apelike than human. But the commanding voice robbed the ape image of reality. This was a man who spoke and others obeyed. The momentary shock he'd experienced on first seeing us vanished.

"You were listed as missing over the Nullarbor," he said. "Presumed dead."

"Just a spot of engine trouble. We had to leave the plane behind and rent a jeep," I said.

"Nick, it wasn't *that* way at all. Why . . ." Daniela started. It was my turn to ram an elbow into her ribs to shut her up. She spun and her brown eyes burned. Daniela finally subsided and let me do the talking. For the moment.

"When Marian called me on the radio, he said you'd be arriving a couple days ago. After an hour past ETA, I did some calling around. No one had heard from you, and a commercial liner had seen a plane going down in flames over the Nullarbor. They presumed it was your plane, from the description and all. . . ."

"Must be some other poor bloke. Nothing that drastic happened. Just a clogged fuel line, but it couldn't be fixed easily. Some of the clog had gotten into the cylinders and fouled them. We decided to go it by truck from Yalata," I explained. All the while I spoke, I carefully watched Marston's expression. The shock vanished and was replaced by a poker face that revealed nothing.

"I'll have your rooms made up. When I heard, well, never mind that," he said brusquely. "You're here now. Marian didn't make it all that clear what you wanted."

"She's doing research into the religious rituals of the aborigines. I'm footing the bill for this little expedition in order to do a series of features on life in Australia."

Marston scowled, then shrugged, as if to say, "It's your money and time you're wasting."

"Come on inside out of the sun. I'll have Claire fix you something to drink."

"Claire?" Daniela asked.

"My daughter. Her mother's dead these last eight months." I heard the anguish in the man's words. He didn't have to tell me how much he'd loved his wife; it rang out clearly in those brief words.

We went inside and were pleasantly surprised by the taste shown in decorating. I suspected Marston hadn't touched a single item in the house since his wife's death—and that she'd been responsible for the way the place looked. He'd be more at home out dipping sheep, not deciding that the fawn brown curtains went well with the pale gold rug.

"Daddy?" came a light, almost lilting voice from the next room. "Who is it?"

Claire Marston came into the room. She was totally out of place on a sheep station. Everything about her hinted at genteel upbringing, a grace and wit belonging more to continental Europe than Australia. Her clothing had a decided Paris-designer look, and her coiffure hadn't been perfected over a tin tub and a bottle of cheap shampoo. Her hair was more of a spun golden fleece than the sandy thatch sported by her father, but the features were definitely his. The small, almost fragile bone structure might have been inherited from her mother but the broad face, the wide-spaced eyes, the aquiline nose, the pursed lips, those were Ram Marston's.

I had to shake myself out of imagining what she'd look like after a week in the sun. The skin would toughen and the lines would form around the eyes from perpetual squinting. She'd look even more like her father then.

"Claire's been back from Swiss finishing school since her mother died. She's been a real help for me. Been hard, Denise dying like that."

"Cancer," said the girl softly, looking at her father. Then, louder, "It's so nice to have visitors. We see so few people, and it's so far into any real city."

"Do you get into Adelaide often?" I asked.

"Only once since I've been back to Australia," the girl answered. "But I've been to Sydney several times."

"We came from there," spoke up Daniela, not one to allow a conversation to pass her by. "And I must say you're quite a sight out here in the desert. We've been with a mob of abos. I can *use* some civilized company. Do tell me what you . . ."

Daniela rattled on while I turned my attention back to Marston. The man smiled slightly, then gestured for me to follow him, leaving the women behind. In a study off the long hallway, he indicated a large, overstuffed chair. I sat.

"Have some whiskey," he offered. I took it and waited. This was his show. Let him do the talking. The whiskey was good. I made sure to roll it around over my tastebuds and savor its smoky flavor before swallowing.

"Good having some female company for Claire," he said at length. "This is no fit place for a woman."

"Is your daughter going back to Switzerland? To finish school?"

"She's done. Hardly looks it, does she? Twenty years old last month. And her mother never even saw her diploma." He took a drink of scotch large enough to choke a horse. The tear welling at the corner of his eye didn't come from the liquor. Here was a man able to hold his booze well.

"This *is* rough country," I said. "The abos Daniela is so hot about studying don't treat their women very well."

"Very well?" snorted Marston. "They're treated like slaves. No fit way to treat ladies. But then, none of them are ladies. Not likely, not with multiple marriages."

"Do you employ many on your station?"

"Not many. They come and go. I usually have about a dozen out rounding up sheep, helping keep up the fences and there's always a bounty for dingoes. Bloody dogs eat more sheep than I shear."

"How big is your station? It's hard to get an idea with the fences vanishing into the distance in every direction."

Marston laughed. "The station's big. More'n a thousand square miles."

"You must be very rich. And this is a nice place."

"Rich," he said, his eyes getting a far-off look. "No, not after Denise's medical bills. Cancer's an expensive disease, Mr. Carter. But I've enough to keep Claire. My own needs are simple. I cut out this section of the Outback thirty years ago and made it all mine. The challenge is what keeps me here, not the money."

I believed him, but something nagged at the back of my mind. I'd need some checking done on Marston before all the pieces fell into place. But I didn't want to ask Sanford Marian for it. Every time I talked with Marian he either told me I was on the wrong track or steered me into non-productive channels. The KGB headquarters raid had been one of the bloodiest and most futile excursions in a long time for me. I didn't want to repeat that.

I wondered if Ram Marston might be enticed into revealing the information I wanted—if Marston even knew it. Looking at his stolid frame, his square shoulders and set mouth, I decided nothing would squeeze any information from this man he didn't want revealed.

There were other ways. I'd use them, if I had to.

EIGHTEEN

Marston showed me to a small room in the back of the house. While it wasn't as spacious as some of the others I'd noticed, it was clean, neat and had an adjoining bath. I went in and looked at myself in the mirror. A weathered face rutted with craggy lines stared back at me. I hadn't realized the dry air and the intense heat had desiccated my skin so much. I splashed water on my face, then cringed. The alkaline bite was almost more than I could take, even with my face turning into a piece of luggage. I ran the water for a while, then tasted it.

The cutting sharpness of alkalinity made my mouth pucker. Again came the message of the desert: Water is scarce. I figured that the drinking water came from separate taps. This was meant for non-drinking uses, like washing, though how such water could help much was beyond me.

I dried off my face, glad of removing at least the surface layer of dirt, then went to the small window at the far end of the room. Looking out presented me with both a marvelous and a marvelously barren view. The rocky ravines, the rolling sand dunes, the occasional clumps of brush and grass all made me think of another planet. Not even the pictures I'd seen of Mars were this alien, though.

Somewhere in that alienness rotated a Soviet radar dish, sucking in signals from military and civilian flights, monitoring vital and non-vital tests from Woomera, even possibly readying to act as a radar beacon for incoming Russian missiles.

I heaved a sigh, adjusted the shoulder holster carrying Wilhelmina and jerked up the window. The wooden screeching made a racket that would awaken the dead. I stopped, waited. No response. I finally jacked the window up enough for me to slip between window and ledge. At least there wasn't any problem with the window falling back down after I'd explored a bit.

The station looked more like a ghost town than a working sheep ranch. While a dozen sheep were penned some distance away, readied for dipping and testing for scabies, from the look of the equipment around, few animals of any description were visible. I glanced around and saw no one, so I pushed on toward the barn.

Inside were five horses, a pair of cows and a pile of feed. Little else in the way of life stirred, though I thought I heard the cackling of chickens.

"Whoa, steady, there," I said to one horse, intent on banging hooves against the wooden stall as I passed. Pressing my hand to a wet nose, I calmed the animal. When the horse snorted and finally decided a few remaining oats in a bucket were more important than I was, I continued my search.

The place looked as if it had been stripped. Little equipment lay about, the animals, while well enough fed, weren't being pampered, and there were damn few of them. The horses seemed a necessary part of a sheep or cattle station in Australia. While Marston had a pair of planes out on the runway, horses would be required for the actual herding of the sheep. I doubted Marston had a helicopter. The runway looked well used by the single engine planes, and there hadn't been a landing pad for a copter.

"Well," I said to myself, "this place is a working station, but only barely. It looks like most of it's already been auctioned off to the highest bidder."

I continued poking about and found nothing more. I decided I needed to look at Marston's books to see what profit this sheep ranch actually turned. In a way, I felt guilty about spying on the man. He had consented to act as host while I pursued some mysterious goal of being a reporter.

He might be a hard-working, innocent man. My suspicious nature wouldn't let me think that, though. Sanford Marian had told Marston that Daniela and I were flying out. Marston could have sabotaged our plane—or had it sabotaged. Whatever had happened to us in the air over the Nullarbor Plains hadn't been an accident.

But why? And did Marian suspect Marston? Was that why he'd chosen this man of all the possible station owners?

Too many questions. I hate it when I don't have the answers. But somehow, Ram Marston triggered suspicion in my unconscious. I have to listen to those warnings. Sometimes, when I'm operating in the dark, they're all I have.

Seldom had I been more in the dark than I was now.

I started back to the main house when I heard angry voices. Hesitating, I turned slowly and finally located the source. From behind the barn came Marston's bass boom. The reply was higher pitched and indecipherable, but the station owner had been berating someone for carelessness. When my name was intermixed with that complaint, I decided to do more than just walk away.

Edging around the barn, I dropped to a crouch and peered around the corner. Ten feet away stood Marston and several of the aborigines from Pierce's tribe. The Pitjandjara manage to make their decorative markings distinctive enough that a non-expert like myself can at least pick out differences in design. I recognized Mickey, in particular, and thought I did two of the others.

"This proper big mess," protested Mickey. "How you want blackfellas to do it?"

It took me a second to figure out Mickey was the one Marston singled out for the criticism. I had difficulty understanding the abos at the best of times. I needed Daniela here to translate even this pidgin English. They changed "f's" to "p's" and had a peculiar way of stringing together the words.

I didn't need any translator for Marston, though.

"Dammit, you black bastard, I paid you already. What the bloody hell do you mean saying you want more for this?"

"More," said one of the others. "Not much."

"Not one bloody shilling more!" ranted Marston. His face turned red and his fists tensed into bony hammers. If I'd been facing him, I don't think I'd have been as cool and collected as the aborigines appeared.

"Ghosts never helped us. You said ghosts would." Mickey crossed his arms and leaned back slightly, the picture of affront.

"You were supposed to take care of this on your own. Now, do it or I'll see you all skinned and hung out on the shed to dry!"

Marston whirled and stalked off, leaving the tiny knot of abos behind. They talked among themselves in their own dialect, but the implications of what they said were plain enough. They'd do as they pleased, and to hell with Ram Marston.

I ducked into the barn as Mickey and the others walked away. While I had no clear idea what Marston had paid them to do—and that they hadn't done—I had a good idea it boded ill for me.

NINETEEN

I picked at my dinner. In the aborigine camp I hadn't been the least fussy. In fact, since it had been my first time eating red kangaroo meat, I'd approached the meal with a sense of adventure. The meal Marston served lacked the adventure—it also lacked the taste.

"I'm not too good a cook," apologized Claire Marston. She dropped her eyes to her plate and seemed to fold in on herself. "The fact is, I'm not too good at many things."

"That's not true!" contradicted Marston. His deep bass reverberated throughout the dining room. "My daughter's too modest. She got top grades at that fancy Swiss school. Top grades."

"They didn't teach me how to cook, Daddy," she said.

Daniela said nothing the whole while this miniature argument flowed back and forth. She simply scooped up the food and forked it into her mouth, eating mechanically. I had the feeling that she'd eat wood pulp and cardboard if it were put in front of her. In the Outback, people can't be too particular about what they eat, and I suspected she'd eaten some pretty vile things in her day.

"I think you've done a good job," I lied. Claire rewarded me with a shy smile that made me uneasy. There was no denying the fact she was a woman. For dinner she wore a simple white blouse tucked into expensive designer jeans that fit like a second skin. The woman's breasts weren't large, but they were ample, her hips were all any man could ask for and her legs were sleek and slender in the tight denim. All that wasn't what caused my discomfort.

It was the naïveté. She was twenty years old, yet acted as demur and innocent as any twelve-year-old. I didn't know what sort of school she'd gone to in Switzerland, but it had obviously kept her cloistered like a nun to the point her emotional development had been stunted.

Physically a woman, I couldn't help but think of Claire Marston as being emotionally a child.

"I don't cook anywhere near as good as Mum did," Claire denied. But the hint of a blush coming to her cheeks told me she was pleased by my simple compliment.

"What you've got there is prime lamb," said Marston, beaming. "Best on the station."

I took the opportunity to ask him about the workings of his ranch.

"Well," he said slowly, "you don't see that much around here because I spread out over the countryside as far as the eye can see. The grass is sparse, and the sheep have to graze a lot of acres to survive."

"What do they do for water?" asked Daniela, peering up from her meal. She only hesitated between mouthfuls before continuing to eat. She was a living, breathing tribute to any food, no matter how bad.

"We have a sophisticated watering system. Pumps, irrigation lines, some underground tubes tapping into very deep artesian wells. But this year's been a bloody bad one. Too dry. Everything's turned into a bone out there."

"It's been getting drier each year," said Claire. "It had been two years since I'd been home. In that time . . ." Her voice trailed off as she remembered the happier times on the station, when her mother had still lived.

"That might make a nice slant for my story," I said, grateful when the maid took away my plate. "Station owners fighting against encroaching desert. Made a good story when I did something similar on the Sahara creeping into the center of Africa."

"Don't play up on it too much," said Marston in clipped tones. His voice carried a sharper edge to it than necessary.

I'd touched a sore spot with him.

"Why not? Everyone loves to read human interest stuff. The valiant station owners against the implaccable drought. That kind of thing builds circulation."

"And spreads lying rumors. We're doing great out here. Just fine." He slammed his fist down so hard on the table that the remaining plates jumped. Even Daniela looked up in surprise. Ram Marston realized how badly he'd reacted, took a deep breath and then excused himself.

We watched him leave. I heard Claire sigh, a sound like air slowly releasing from a tire valve.

"He's under considerable pressure since Mum died," she said in a weak voice. "There's nothing I can do to help, either."

"Help?" I asked. "How do you mean?"

"I can't cook. I'm at a loss to do the things that Mum found so easy. The hired help is loyal enough but have been drifting away over the past few years. The station is dying."

"The drought?"

"Yes," she said, the word almost inaudible. She rose quickly and said, "Please excuse me. I know I'm a terrible hostess but . . ."

"Don't worry about us, dear," said Daniela. "We can find our way around just fine." Claire gave her a smile that combined both relief and sorrow, then left.

Daniela waited until the other woman had left before saying, "She's a nice kid. Seems a pity wasting her out here in the Outback."

"She's trying too hard to fill her mother's shoes. She's been trained for other things."

"Oh, so you noticed, Nick?" asked Daniela, her brows arching. "I didn't think womanly wiles meant anything to you."

"Whatever gave you that idea?" I asked. "I simply melt whenever a lovely lady bats her eyelashes at me—like you're doing now."

Daniela laughed delightedly.

"You're such a tease, Nick. And such an enigma."

I didn't press the point. The less Daniela thought about

me and the more she concentrated on her research the more I liked it.

Night came with surprising suddenness in the desert. One minute, the sun beat down with a ferocity unmatched in the world, the next the cool winds threatened to freeze the meat on your bones. I pulled my jacket around me as I stood at the corner of the house. The few servants inside the house had finished their chores and were heading for bed. The three or four ranch hands entrusted with tending the sheep had already done their work and had left for their quarters some distance away. I'd checked out their quarters earlier and found them to be similar to a military barracks. For this country, that seemed like luxury.

The aborigines camped over two miles away, and Daniela had gone off with tape recorder and camera to record the doings of their "proper big business *corroboree*. She'd urged me to come along and I had—for about a half mile.

"I've got to go back," I'd said. "I forgot something."

"But Nick," Daniela had protested, "without me you can't get into the ceremony. Once it starts, they don't allow anyone in."

"Then you'll have to take good pictures so I'll know what I missed." The truth was I *did* want to see the ceremony. But finding the location of the Soviets radar installation took top priority.

"Oh, you!" she'd said in exasperation. She reached over and pulled my head down so she could kiss me. Then Daniela Rhys-Smith was off, humming an aborigine ditty to herself as she tromped on down the road to the ceremonial site.

I watched until she vanished into the distance, then cut off across the desert. Orienting myself by the stars proved easier now since I'd had time to study them. While there wasn't a counterpart to the North Star, the constellations themselves gave me enough hint of direction so I wouldn't easily become lost.

Returning to the house, I prowled around until all the lights inside winked off. Then I began my search in earnest. The barn hadn't given me any clues earlier. It wouldn't now. I concentrated on a slowly widening area starting at the house and moving in slow circles. Every inch of the ground received at least a cursory glance.

Nothing.

I'd hoped to find evidence of heavy trucks, of something that might have brought in large quantities of food or electronic equipment adequate to supply a radar station. Everywhere I looked gave me back the same answer: nothing.

Still, the winds blew strongly in this part of the desert, the sheep with their cloven hooves chopped up the terrain and any such transport of material might have taken place months ago. This gloomy outlook didn't prevent me from working my way out until I came to the radio shack.

The tall antenna weaved about in the brisk wind, bending down like an old man and singing a mournful contralto song through the thick steel guy wires. I worked my way forward, careful not to move in any way that would attract the attention of anyone looking out the single window on the side of the shed.

Peering inside gave me no hint of anything wrong. A single grimy light bulb dangling on a bare wire hung from the ceiling. The radio shack was empty. I tried the door, found it unlocked. I slipped inside, grateful for the respite from the stinging wind. Bits of sand had started kicking up and felt like some unseen hand trying to sandpaper the skin off my face.

A fine layer of grit covered everything inside. I checked the logbook beside the transmitter and found that the last transmission had been only an hour before, yet the sand had already sifted down on the chair, the desktop, the transmitter itself.

Looking over the various logged transmissions told me little; there were a few to a store in Alice Springs, about a dozen in the past month to Sydney—nothing suspicious. I sat down in the chair and simply stared at the radio.

There had to be something I was missing. Ram Marston

had chewed out the aborigines over some failure; probably their abortive attempt to kill me. He'd known about Daniela's and my flight here. That made him a prime suspect in that sabotage. The station was slowly failing, yet Marston appeared prosperous. That might mean outside money coming in, money from Russian sources in exchange for hiding the radar station.

And yet again, it might all mean nothing. The evidence I had was worse than tenuous; it was nonexistent. All I had against Marston were hunches.

Leaning back in the chair almost toppled me over. One of the legs had loosened. I caught myself and turned to get all four legs back on the dirty wood floor. In the process a white flash caught my eye. I bent over and retrieved the crumpled piece of paper tossed into the corner of the room.

Unfolding it and smoothing it, I saw the smeary line written in pencil. It was a single number, but it provided me with the first real link between Marston and the Soviets.

The number corresponded to a frequency often used by their field agents to contact trawlers off the coast of the U.S. I had no reason to doubt that the Russians used the same frequency in other parts of the world. If so, someone had contacted a Soviet vessel.

Marston?

There wasn't any proof, but the noose drew a little tighter.

"What are you doing here?" came the soft inquiry. In spite of the lowness of tone and the mildness of the voice, I jumped. One smooth movement pulled the scrap of paper from in front of me and shoved it deep into a jacket pocket. Only then did I turn to face Claire Marston.

"I wanted to see the radio room. This is quite a setup. Do you know how to use it?"

"No, not really. Do you?" she asked, her wide-set green eyes innocent and unaccusing.

I took a deep breath and relaxed.

"I've used similar rigs. When I was covering a story in Africa recently, I had to use something like this. But about all I know how to do is turn the set on and off. If the frequency isn't already set for me, I'm lost."

"Oh?" she said, still in that little-girl voice. "I can do a bit more than that. Here, let me show you." She leaned past me, acting as if she didn't realize her breasts brushed across my upper arm. Claire turned on the set, let it warm, then proudly said, "It's set for transmission to Sydney."

"Call there often?" I asked.

She blushed, which wasn't the response I'd thought I'd get.

"Not really." The woman averted her eyes, looking back at the radio.

I didn't tell her I'd looked through the logbook and knew that was a lie. The calls to Sydney had been entered in a different hand, one using a lighter pressure on the pen. Claire had made the calls and now went out of her way to deny it.

"Then, Mr. Carter," she said, continuing as if I hadn't upset her, "all you do is press down on the button when you wish to speak. I suppose this is familiar to you, if you've used a field radio before."

"Yes," I said, not moving. She stayed very close to me. I inhaled and my nose twitched slightly at the subtle fragrance of her perfume. It was definitely European and out of place in the Outback.

"It's my only link to civilization," she continued, in a tone like a drowning man might use. She floundered about, waiting for me to come to her rescue.

"You're very lonely out here, aren't you? No one but your father, and he's not the kind of company a lady educated in Switzerland would choose on her own."

"I love Daddy!" she protested.

"I know," I said quietly, "but you hate the station. You hate the Outback. You don't belong here."

"Oh, Mr. Carter . . ."

"Nick," I corrected.

"Nick, I feel so trapped. I'm going insane out here. I grew up here, but my life's in Europe now, not in the middle of the desert."

Her face was near mine. I reached out and touched her cheek. The warmth turned hotter under my fingertips. She crushed her lips against mine with surprising passion. I returned the kiss. Locked up inside her was a woman's passion, a passion thwarted by her isolation. Lurking under her mild manner was a hot-blooded siren's desires, probably cultivated in Europe and now dying in Australia.

My arms circled her trim body. Claire looked fragile, but her body did everything possible to deny it. Our bodies moved together in a twisting, turning, demanding motion that would have crushed a truly fragile creature. She was resilient, vital, all-woman.

I felt her hands lacing through my hair as we kissed. At her insistence, my kisses worked downward—to the point of her chin, to the hollow of her white neck, lower. Magically, the buttons on her white blouse came loose one by one. She didn't wear a bra. Warm, firm flesh flowed under my wet kisses.

Sucking one taut nipple into my mouth brought a gasp of pure joy from her lips. I knew then that there wasn't any denying our emotions now. The die was cast.

Claire moved around so that she perched on the edge of the table, her fingers already pulling down those skin-tight jeans. Her legs parted in a decidedly unladylike manner as she pulled me into her.

"Don't treat me like I'm a porcelain doll, Nick darling," she whispered hotly in my ear. "I won't break. I promise."

"This isn't the first time you've done this, is it?" The question was purely rhetorical. No fainting virgin responded so surely, so knowingly. She'd learned more in Europe than how to make small talk at an afternoon tea.

I moved into the vee of her slender legs, feeling her hand guiding me to the target we both sought so avidly. She lifted up off the table and wiggled forward slightly, then we both gasped in unison as I buried myself to the hilt.

In tempo with the howling wind outside, we made love. Claire's shrieks of joy were turned back, thwarted, muffled by the wind, but her passion soared ever higher. When we were finished, I held her tight, gently rocking her to and fro like I would a small child.

"It might sound clichéd but I really needed that," Claire

said. "I'm going wonky thinking what life will be like out here."

"You don't owe your father. Move into Sydney or Melbourne. Go back to Europe."

"I . . . I can't. I feel so sorry for him. Mum was everything to him. He's still taking her death so hard I feel I ought to do what I can to ease his pain."

"He can't make a slave out of you to ease his pain," I pointed out. "You have your own life to live. A beautiful woman can wilt out here in the desert."

"Like Daniela Rhys-Smith?" she asked.

"Don't be catty. Daniela lives for her research. She's doing what she wants. You should, too."

"Oh, Nick, I don't know what to do. I love my father. But I'm so lonely!"

She buried her face in my shoulder. I felt hot tears touching my skin and, as I inhaled, I caught the exotic perfume in her hair.

I'd smelled that perfume before. On Sanford Marian.

TWENTY

I slept fitfully, awakened several times during the night by the wild dogs baying at the moon. Just before the first light of dawn, I dressed and slipped out the window again, heading for the radio shack. I thanked my lucky stars Marston had placed it far enough away from the main house so that my trip would probably go unnoticed. In spite of the early hour, I approached the shed cautiously, making sure no one was inside.

The last thing in the world I wanted now was to blow my cover. It was tenuous enough without my actions causing Marston to become even more suspicious.

Sitting in front of the rig, I let it warm up. The cold night air chilled me to the bone. The welcome hum of the transmitter soon brought a bit of warmth to the shed. This wasn't a modern radio in any sense of the word. Old-style tubes inside gave off enough heat to melt butter.

As I reached to turn the dial to contact Sanford Marian, I noticed that it was already set on the proper frequency. Frowning, I picked up the microphone and tapped the transmit button a couple times. The squawk of static greeted me.

"Come in N19 . . . this is N3 . . . over," I said slowly, distinctly. When I repeated the call, a harsher roar of static sounded from the tinny speakers.

"Go ahead, N3," came Marian's voice. "How are you doing in the great Australian Outback?"

"I'm not making any progress," I said, choosing my

words with care. I felt as if I had been dumped into the middle of a shooting gallery and the passing crowd was being allowed to take potshots at me for ten cents a bullet.

"I told you so, old chap," came Marian's cheery words. "Do you intend to return to Sydney any time soon?"

"Can't leave immediately," I replied, "because of my cover. If I don't try to do *some* reporter-type work, Marston will become suspicious. I shouldn't be longer than another day, though. Why do you ask?"

I wished I'd been in the same room with Marian. The way a man's eyes move, the set of his mouth, the way he holds his body, all this tells more than simple words. Even worse, the static drowned out any of the subtler nuances in the man's words. He might as well have slipped a note under the door for the information I got.

"Think I tracked down the source of that abo. The one that tried to do you in."

"Wasn't he Pitjandjara?"

"No, he belonged to the Wanindiljaugwa tribe."

"Where are they located?"

"Seems they're to be found in northern Australia, old chap," came Marian's confident words. "You might want to go on up to Groote and see if you can get a line from there."

"I'll probably return to Sydney first," I told him.

My mind raced. Things simply didn't fit together in any way that made sense. Sanford Marian was an AXE agent, yet I had detected Claire Marston's perfume on his clothing. For so much to be absorbed, it had to mean more than a casual passing in the street.

Marian and Claire seeing one another would explain a good deal, particularly how Marian happened to know of the Marston station. Their affair might have nothing to do with the Soviet radar station; in fact, it seemed unlikely it did.

Enter one additional fact: Ram Marston had been furious with the aborigines from Pierce's tribe. While I hadn't figured out fully what the row was about, it sounded as if he berated them for not permanently removing me from the game. And, no matter what Marian said, the abo who'd tried to spear me in Sydney had been a Pitjandjara. I trusted Daniela Rhys-Smith's opinion in that matter.

Or should I trust her at all?

I shook my head. Such rampant paranoia got me nowhere.

"I'll be expecting you in a day or two, then. I'll save my full report for your arrival."

"It'll be good getting back to civilization," I said. "Out." I heard the pop indicating Marston had cut his receiver off. I flipped off the power switch and sat back, thinking hard. The waters had become even more muddied. I cursed Hawk for giving me this assignment, then hurried back to the main house before anyone missed me.

I slid back through the open window and sat in the shadows for a moment, wondering why the uneasiness I felt increased until I wanted to scream. I checked my Lüger, then rose and went to the door. I pressed my ear against the heavy wood panel and listened. Faint sounds echoed down the hallway, but nothing alarming. Opening the door a crack, I peered out.

Nothing.

While it might have been my imagination or my inability to figure out how best to complete my mission, I doubted it. This feeling had a substantial goad to it. I moved down the hall until I came to Daniela's door. Trying the knob and finding it unlocked, I silently went into her room.

It was empty.

I frowned when I didn't see any of her equipment, either. I doubted she had stayed with the aborigines all night. The *corroboree,* from her explanation, shouldn't have lasted more than a few hours. Pressing my hand down on the still-made bed, I felt only coldness. It hadn't been slept in.

I spun at the sound of shoe soles in the hall. Wilhelmina vanished into her holster in time to keep Ram Marston from seeing the weapon.

"Mr. Carter," he said in his gruff, deep voice. "Looking for Dr. Rhys-Smith?"

"She doesn't seem to be here," I said cautiously, not wanting to give away anything.

"She's left already."

"Left?" I didn't have to feign surprise.

"She got back from the abo wingding, packed and left."

"How? The Land Rover's still out front." I almost bit my tongue when I uttered those words. If I'd just gotten up, there wasn't any way I could have seen the truck and known it was still parked by the barn.

Marston didn't seem to notice my slip.

"Plane came for her. One of the university blokes radioed in, said something about her meeting with the dean and how her position at the university depended on it. I saw her off."

"Well, I'd been depending on her to fill me in on some of the background rituals practiced by the Pitjandjara."

"Pitjandjara?" said Marston. Then he laughed. "You pick up the lingo fast, I'll give you that, Mr. Carter. Around here, we just call them abos and don't bother with placing them in their tribes."

"Pitjandjara, Wanindiljaugwa, such colorful names," I said, watching Marston's reaction. He tensed slightly. I pressed further. "I'd meant to get most of my story here before going on to Groote."

"You reporters do end up in out of the way spots," declared Marston. "But come along and have breakfast. Claire's asking about you. Seems she's taken quite a shine to you, but then I suspect that's only natural. She's not got any friends near her age out here."

"She ought to get into the city more often. I'm sure she'd enjoy Sydney."

"Why do you say that?" I might have scalded the man with boiling water.

I shrugged and answered, "It seemed like a nice city to me as I passed through. Miss Marston's used to continental sophistication, and Sydney would come closer than a sheep station. Isn't that so?"

"Yes, yes," he said, hurrying along.

I followed, barely able to keep up the pace. Marston's shoulders hunched forward, and he looked like a chimpanzee ready to swing from a tree. I vowed again to be very careful around the man. The years of living out on the edge of civilization had hardened and strengthened him. Ram Marston would be a formidable opponent in a fight.

And I knew now it would come to that. His reactions to the names mentioned by Sanford Marian told me all I needed to know, even if I hadn't become suspicious concerning Daniela's disappearance. I'm a light sleeper and hadn't heard any plane take off or land during the night. In addition, I had been out prowling around most of that time. The hour Marston indicated Daniela had left was when Claire and I were in the radio shack. The wind might have muffled some of an airplane's engine noise, but not that much.

Whatever had happened to Daniela Rhys-Smith, she hadn't left the station via airplane. She was being used as a catspaw in a more deadly game than recording aborigine religious beliefs. But if Marston thought this gave him a hold over me, he was wrong.

As much as I cared for Daniela, the mission came first. Always.

TWENTY-ONE

I spent the day with Claire following me around as if she were a giddy teenager in love for the first time. No matter how I tried to get free to do my job of spying, she followed too closely.

"Tell me all about Washington, Nick," she asked as I walked toward the spot where the aborigines had held their ceremony the night before. I hoped to find some evidence showing that Daniela hadn't been called back but rather had been kidnapped.

"Dirty city. I don't much like it. I prefer New England much more. I have a small place up in Vermont."

"On a lake?" she asked eagerly.

"I enjoy fishing," I told her, nodding assent in answer to her question. "The winters are great there, too. Lots of snow. I'm not too far from some ski slopes."

"I learned to ski at St. Moritz," she said, a faraway look coming into her eyes. I felt her leaving and going back to her school days in Switzerland. They'd obviously been far happier times for her than her existence out here on the sheep ranch.

"I've been to St. Moritz," I said. "There's a lot of travel on this job. That's one reason I enjoy it."

"It seems so . . . romantic being a reporter for a magazine," she sighed.

"Newspaper," I corrected. I had to keep my cover story straight.

"You must be sent to all the fun spots in the world."

"All the trouble spots, too. I was in Guatemala and got shot at." I decided to try a different tact when I saw her response. Claire's eyes widened and turned into green pools of awe. I wanted her to do something else besides tag along with me like a homeless puppy dog.

I laughed ruefully and added, "There was a camera man with me. He was loading his gun and it went off. That was the closest I've ever come to being shot, and it was by my own side."

"A camera man carried a weapon?"

"This one did. Against orders, of course, but he was a strange one. All the time going on about how he'd been a Green Beret in Nam. He hadn't even been in the military." I turned and studied the terrain—in time to see a blond head duck behind a clump of trees some distance away.

An aborigine followed us.

"Still, travelling to those countries must be thrilling," Claire continued in her breathless manner.

"It gets dull living out of a suitcase. Take this assignment. Desert heat, no water, bugs everywhere." The gnats followed me like I carried a homing device. Every time I opened my mouth a few more slipped inside. Spitting did little good and, hardened as I am, swallowing didn't seem like all that great an idea.

"It can't be too bad," the woman said, her hand resting lightly on my arm. "We met."

I shrugged, as if saying that I always met women. Claire pulled her hand away and turned from me.

I stooped while she continued on up a rise and examined the road. An empty film canister lay half-buried. Checking it confirmed my suspicion. It was one of Daniela's. Still, it proved nothing. According to Marston, the woman had gone back to the station before receiving the message to leave. This could have been dropped on her return trip.

Feeling that locating Daniela provided a significant key to the problem facing me kept me going. The mission came first, but it looked more and more like rescuing Daniela and destroying the radar station could be accomplished in one fell swoop.

I had to make several unsavory conjectures, but I made them.

Ram Marston was implicated in the Soviet's scheme. His daughter and Marian were intimately entangled. Whether Claire siphoned knowledge from an unwitting Marian or if this were incidental, I didn't know yet. The coincidence of Marston being involved with the radar station—and Daniela's kidnapping—and Sanford Marian sending me out here struck me as unreal. I had to identify the players on the other side before I moved.

Ram Marston definitely counted as an enemy. Claire might or might not. The thought intruded that our lovemaking the night before might have other motives than loneliness and mutual attraction. She might have instigated it to keep me occupied while Daniela was removed. And even Daniela Rhys-Smith might be on the opposite side. While I strongly doubted it, the possibility was one I didn't dare overlook.

That left the even more confusing status of Sanford Marian. He was an AXE agent, a damned good one with an enviable track record. On the other hand, Hawk had seen fit to send me in without telling Marian. An agent of Marian's caliber should have been able to handle this assignment easily enough; he hadn't even progressed as far as I already had in just a few days.

Or had he?

Was he playing some other game? Had he and Hawk come to some agreement about which I knew nothing, just as Hawk had sent me in without telling Marian? Even more vexing was the knowledge that Elaine Thompson wasted time counting penguins off the coast of New Zealand. That was high-powered backup for a simple search and destroy mission, if she were a backup.

If this were a simple search and destroy.

"Damn," I said, flinging a rock to the ground. A tiny puff of dust kicked up and immediately fell back, half covering the rock.

"What's wrong, Nick?" came Claire's voice from the top of the dune.

"Nothing," I said.

On my way up, I spotted two more of the aborigines. I thought one of them might be Mickey, but I couldn't be sure at this distance. What did seem assured was the fact that they followed us. It wasn't much of a leap to decide that Ram Marston had sent them to watch me.

I'd told Marston I'd leave in the morning. This satisfied the man but made it more difficult for me. Either I found what I wanted tonight or I had to set up a camp at some distance and spend a good deal of my time hiding in the desert. I didn't know if I was up to that or not.

Two abos paced around the house. Sentries. Waiting until they had gone by on their round, I slipped out once again. I felt as if I pioneered a brand-new highway into the desert. I used the window more than the door to leave my tiny room in the Marston house.

Claire had kept me from doing any substantive checking today, but prior to this I'd pretty well determined the layout of the station. The barn and house were built on bedrock, an outjutting of flint so hard it'd take tons of dynamite to blast into it. But the radio shack was some distance away. This struck me as curious, even before I found the scrap of paper with the Russian contact frequency written on it.

It wasn't so curious if Marston didn't want occasional visitors to the transmitter being seen by anyone in the house. It might be especially embarrassing if those occasional visitors spoke only Russian.

I watched for some minutes to make certain the aborigines hadn't detected my leaving the house. When sure that they continued their slow pacing, I jogged out to the radio shack. The transmitter shed wasn't constructed on flint rock like the house, but enough rock croppings poked through the desert nearby to convince me that underneath wasn't purely sand.

Walking in ever-widening circles, examining the ground as I went, revealed nothing.

I found the entrance by accident.

In a rock upthrust I noticed deeper shadows than expected. I reached out to see what type of stone it was. My hand came away with a slight paint odor on it. Checking closer, I found someone had painted the rock black to enhance the darkness. I moved along the rock face, found it turned into a hidden doorway before descending into the bowels of the Australian desert.

The rock on either side had been scraped and nicked recently, another reason it had been painted over where it could be seen easily. The metallic slashes told me the story. Marston had gone to too much trouble to hide this for it to be anything legal.

I bet it led to the Soviet's radar unit.

As I groped about in the dark, I found a circular ramp spiralling downward. Wilhelmina came to my hand, and I felt ready to tackle the entire Russian army.

At the foot of the ramp, some fifty feet underground, a dim light showed the way. I hadn't taken five steps when I heard the grunts of men coming down behind me. I sprinted down the hall—and ran headlong into a Russian sergeant.

TWENTY-TWO

The Russian soldier was more startled than I was. We went down in a tangle of arms and kicking legs. I landed on top.

"*Shto ehtah znahcheet?*" he demanded. Carrying on a long discussion as to how I happened to be in a secret Soviet installation buried beneath the Australian Outback didn't seem the right thing to do. I slugged him with the butt of my Luger.

The soldier groaned, then slumped. And the footsteps coming down the spiral entryway came closer and closer.

Cursing, I got my feet under me and kicked open the nearest door. Dragging the sergeant inside took longer than I'd intended. I barely slammed the door behind us when the two aborigines who'd been guarding the Marston house stalked by. They didn't seem the least bit curious about the noise I'd made subduing the soldier and getting him into the room.

Maybe the ways of the whitefellas confused them as much as their ways did "civilized" men.

Panting, I leaned against the door while they continued on their way. Only when I'd regained my breath did I bother to look around. Luck had been with me. I'd picked a storeroom to do my hiding.

The shelves sagged under electronic gear stacked willy-nilly on them. Russian Cyrillic characters written on masking tape marked the various piles. Turning from the room to the man I'd knocked out, I first examined his insignia. While he wore a Russian uniform, all unit insignia had been removed. He was a sergeant in the Red Army, nothing more. If anyone happened to come on this place and alert the Australian authorities, the people manning the radar station could never be tried as spies. The worst that could happen would be a stern message to the Soviets and deportation for the technicians.

Given any kind of warning, I suspected the sergeant and the others buried under the desert could destroy the radar unit totally, making any charges against them little more than illegal entry into the country.

This planting of radar units in Western countries seemed virtually risk-free for the Russians.

I'd have to change that.

I stripped off the man's shirt, ripped it into strips and tied him securely. As a final touch, a dirty handkerchief went into his mouth and was firmly fastened there. If he didn't have adenoids, he'd live. Otherwise, he might suffocate. That was a chance we'd both have to take.

Looking out into the hall and seeing no one provided the goad to get moving. Walking along slowly, checking the doors, I found a complete machine shop, an electronics repair facility and a small library, all deserted. The Russians had set up a base and obviously planned to be here for quite a while.

As I looked into another room apparently used as a conference room, I heard low voices approaching. This time I didn't duck out of sight fast enough.

"Hey, whitefella stop!" cried one of the abos.

I turned, paused, then grabbed the man's shoulders when he came close enough. Doubling up, I planted my right foot in his belly and shoved my left between his legs, all the while falling backward. The aborigine cartwheeled over my head to smash into the wall behind. Air gusted from his lungs. It'd be long minutes before he would regain any fight.

But using the judo throw had placed me in an uncomfortable position. On my back, I looked up at the other abo.

We both recognized each other instantly.

"Mickey!" I cried.

"Nick," he said, in a voice that combined sadness with triumph. He lifted his spear to make the final plunge into my guts.

Twisting frantically, I managed to lock my left foot behind his ankle and kick his knee with the right. Mickey jerked off balance, his spear missing me by a fraction of an inch. By the time I'd regained my feet, so had Mickey. We faced each other.

"We're related," I said. "Relatives don't kill each other."

"I kill brother when he kill our father," the aborigine told me. The flint knife between us told the story. The abos lived in a fierce culture where virtually everyone claimed some relation to everyone else. Killing relatives meant nothing to him; it had simply kept him from killing me out of hand as a stranger when we'd first met.

The muscles on my right forearm tensed. I felt my stiletto race forth and land in my grip. While Hugo's blade is of the finest Sheffield steel, I worried about it striking the flint knife. I'd seen even good steel broken by flint.

Mickey circled, making tiny feints with his point. When he attacked, it came in a flurry of motion, half to confuse, half to kill. I barely succeeded in grabbing his thick wrist and forcing aside the knife point driving for my heart. I felt his fingers tighten around my right wrist to keep my knife from similarly burying itself.

It turned into a battle of strength. Almost a foot taller, the product of hard training and good nutrition, the contest had to go to me. And it did.

The aborigine made a tiny gulping noise as the blade slipped between his ribs, then the man smiled and said, "You plenny good whitefella. See you in Dreaming." Then he died.

I gently eased him to the floor and turned to where his companion stirred on the floor. A short, hard jab knocked the abo out. I spent another few minutes tying him up and left both the living and the dead behind.

Continuing my exploration of the underground facility revealed all I needed to know. Opening one door slowly, I peered in. Apparently, the Russians had found a natural canyon, put their radar unit in it under a protective plastic dome, then built the extensive system of storerooms I'd just explored.

Burying the entire radar rig like this cut off some of the peripheral pickup, but not that much. What they lost in information they gained in secrecy.

A half dozen technicians worked at the base of the radar unit, tearing into the electronic guts to repair some small malfunctioning circuit. I shut the door and turned my attention back into the rabbit warren of rooms.

When I found a room with another pair of abos standing guard outside it, I knew I'd found Daniela. The mission came together just as I'd hoped. Destroying the radar unit would be a piece of cake—and I'd get Daniela out, too.

I never heard the blow that knocked me to my knees and sent the world spinning before my eyes.

TWENTY-THREE

I crashed forward, partially supported by the rock wall forming the tunnel. Another blow landed on my shoulders, driving me down further. I twisted and blindly lashed out with my feet, feeling a kneecap crunch as I kicked.

"Bloody hell!" came the immediate cry. I kept kicking as I struggled to regain my senses. My first instinct was to draw Wilhelmina, but that might prove my undoing. Without a clear head and a good target, the gun would be more dangerous for me than my intended victim.

Scooting along, finding the far wall and turning my back to it, I cleared my vision and saw Ram Marston doubled over, clutching his injured knee. The blow hadn't been hard enough to be more than painful. I wished I'd been able to break his kneecap. That would have taken him out of action permanently.

"Get him, you bloody fools!" the man raged.

The two aborigines separated and advanced on me, one on either side of the tunnel. My Luger leaped into my hand, ready for action—until the gutteral command in Russian froze me.

I looked past the abo and saw a Soviet officer holding an assault rifle. I could kill the abo and it'd do no good. The Russian would have a clear field of fire then. There was no question he'd use it to deadly advantage.

"Okay," I said, slowly lifting my hands, Wilhelmina still in my right. The closest aborigine took the gun and peered at it. I doubt if they'd seen its likes out in the desert. All the weapons they carried looked like leftovers from the days of the British Empire. The abos' most modern pistol had been a battered Smith & Wesson Police Positive. To find a Luger would be the same as discovering water.

"Keep it," said Marston to the native. "And he's got a knife on him, too. He killed Mickey with it."

With both Wilhelmina and Hugo gone, I felt naked. Pierre still rested on my inner right thigh, but to use a poison gas capsule now didn't seem the most effective use of the weapon. A stiff breeze gusted down the hallway toward the radar room. This wind would rob the gas grenade of its potency. I had to save it for use when it counted most.

"I hoped you'd buy my story about that bitch leaving to go back to Sydney," said Marston, still rubbing his knee. "You should have pushed off, you bloody fool. Now you're both going to die."

I rose, looking for the opening to land one good blow to the station owner's Adam's apple. The Russian officer wasn't about to let that happen. I felt the cold bore of the AK-47 against my ribs.

"Tell your pet soldier to cool it. I've surrendered. I'm not going anywhere."

Marston's laugh was ugly. "That's truer than you know, Mr. Carter. This will be your grave. Put him in with her."

One of the abos opened the door to the storeroom while the Russian shoved me inside. For a moment, I was blind. There wasn't any light inside, and all I saw was velvet darkness just as if I'd walked into a movie theater.

"Watch it, you bloody bloke!" came the protest as I tripped over something soft on the floor.

"Daniela?" I asked.

"Nick!"

Strong arms circled my neck. I felt lips crush into mine. She obviously had adapted to the darkness.

When she released me, my sight had adjusted to the dimness. I glanced around. It was pretty much as I'd feared. The room had been stripped so that nothing useful remained.

"Why'd you get yourself caught?" she demanded. As usual, she took me offguard with her questions.

"It wasn't planned that way," I heard myself say. "Marston must have noticed I'd slipped away from the house. He sent his two abos after me. I killed Mickey."

"Oh," she said, her voice small.

"When they didn't report back, Marston came looking. And found me. At least, that's the way I think it went down. What about you?"

"Damnedest thing, Nick," she said, dropping to sit tailor fashion on the cold dirt floor. "I'd finished recording the *corroboree* and had made definite arrangements with Pierce to film another in just a few days. He told me their *ngura*—temporary camp—would be moved a few miles to the east for this one. Oh, Nick, it was super! The . . ."

"Daniela, please. What happened to *you*?"

"Sorry, Nick. Even now, I get carried away thinking about my work." She took a deep breath and settled herself. I took the opportunity to make a quick circuit of the room. Nothing.

"As I was saying," she went on, "I walked along the road back to Marston's house when two abos jumped me. Well, I wasn't about to let *that* happen. I fought."

"You dropped an empty film canister," I said. "That's what convinced me you'd been kidnapped."

"Why?" she asked, genuinely curious.

"That had to be either a spare or the canister for the film in your camera. Since you bought both film and camera in Yalata, you didn't have a spare to drop. So, I figured you wouldn't be so careless as to lose the canister."

"Might have."

"You're compulsive about putting things away. It's the anthropologist in you."

"You saw my office. It's a mess."

"I also saw your notes. They're meticulous."

"Point made. Anyway, they brought me here. Wherever that is."

I told her, then added, "It's hiding a Russian radar station."

"I overheard Marston talking about that." I became all ears, hanging on the woman's every word. When she saw this, she hurried on with the explanation. "He wants more money from the Russians for the use of his land. He's almost bankrupt, Nick. The Russians are keeping this station going with their bribe money."

"I figured something like that. There were never any hands around, except for the aborigines."

"They were transients, for the most part," she cut in.

"Right. That's what I thought. Marston won't part with the station because it's his only link to his dead wife. He has nothing but memories left."

"He has his daughter."

"No," I said slowly, "I don't think so. Marston saw how they'd grown apart. She doesn't belong in the Outback anymore. She's European, not Australian. He made the deal with the Soviets to hang onto the sheep ranch."

"There aren't that many Russians in here," said Daniela. "I heard Marston say something about there only being ten. He has nothing at all to do with the running of the unit."

Such an easy search and destroy and I'd botched it. Only ten Soviet soldiers, and all technicians, not fighters. This place should have been dust by now, if I'd done my job right. As it was, I'd ended up endangering Daniela's life and, even worse, probably failing in my mission.

"Daniela," I said suddenly, "talk to the bushmen outside the door. See if you can't convince them to let us go. You speak their language. That should have some weight with them."

"Who are they?"

"I don't know their names," I replied, "but they have to be members of Pierce's mob."

"All the abos around here are Pitjandjara," she said. "Well, it *never* hurts to try." Daniela went to the door and rapped three times on it. An answering grunt told her the aborigines were there. She began rattling on in their language until the sounds blurred together in my ears. The language, she'd told me earlier, was simple. These were

Stone Age people, but the pronunciation proved very difficult for anyone by one of the hard-caked dirt walls.

"It's no good. I don't know what Marston has promised them but they won't even listen to me. I promised them everything from money to guns to religious secrets I've acquired over the years. Nothing worked. Oh, Nick, what are we going to do? They'll kill you, you know. Th-they'll kill m-me!"

She clutched at me, sobbing. I didn't have the foggiest idea what we were going to do. At the moment it looked like our only option was to die.

That didn't please me at all.

TWENTY-FOUR

"They'll kill us," sobbed Daniela. "I know they will."

I didn't say anything. What she said was right. There wasn't anyway in hell that Marston could allow us to live. We'd seen too much, and beyond that, he had to know I was an undercover agent for the United States. He might not know I was an AXE agent, but that made little difference in the long run.

I paced about like a caged tiger. Once, when they came to give us food, I positioned myself beside the door. The instant it opened, I pounced. It didn't do either the aborigine I tackled or me any good. My weight carried the small man out into the corridor, but the other bushman easily subdued me with his spear. A quick poke in the ribs was all it took to make me realize I didn't really want to pursue the fight.

"Nick," said Daniela after my attempt, "who are you?"

"Which story do you want?"

"The truth."

"The truth's too slippery. Besides, I'm not used to telling it in its unvarnished entirety."

"You really *are* a spy, aren't you?"

"Make me into anything you want."

"You said you killed Mickey. There was remorse in your voice, but the act didn't shock you. You actually *killed* another human being and kept right on, as if it didn't count."

"Sure, it counted," I said tiredly. "I liked him. Hell, we'd already agreed we were related."

"But that didn't stop you from shooting him."

"I used my knife." A tiny gasp escaped from her lips. I didn't try to make out her expression in the dark. "He tried to kill me," I said, but the explanation sounded lame.

"You're bigger, stronger. These are small people, these abos. He didn't have a chance."

I didn't want to debate whether it was better to have killed Mickey in a fight or tried to talk him out of stabbing me in the gut. I felt as if I spun my wheels here, that some minor element eluded me and that element spelled the difference between death and finishing off my assignment.

Always, the assignment. Still, it gave purpose to my life and kept me from giving up. To quit now meant death. Nick Carter, Killmaster, never gave up. Ever.

My fingers worked along the seams around the door. No way of escaping there. Someone had carefully reinforced that wall in such a way that a cutting torch might not make much impression. The adjoining wall to the right was pure flint. Not even dynamite would faze it. The rear wall gave little cause for joy, but the other wall presented interesting possibilities.

My fingers crumbled some of the dirt from around heavy stones. Digging out didn't strike me as too likely in this rocky terrain, but I had to give it a try. And try I did. My fingers bled and I lost a fingernail, but an hour's work produced the first real result.

"Daniela, help me," I called.

"What are you doing, Nick? I can't see."

"Digging. A lot."

"I tried already. It's useless."

"Not if you help me with this stone." Together we heaved and tugged and finally pulled it free. A gust of cold air struck me in the face. I laughed and hugged Daniela.

"Nick!" she sobbed. "There's enough room to get through!"

There wasn't, but the way had begun to open.

"Keep digging," I ordered. "We can be out of here in nothing flat."

It took an hour to enlarge the hole to where I slid

through. Then I went exploring, telling Daniela to remain
behind. Until I knew where I was going, I didn't want her
getting in the way.

I'd emerged from the storeroom into a partially completed office. The Russians hadn't finished work here yet,
and the room remained roughly hewn from the living
stone. I saw how lucky we'd been. If the storeroom had
been a few feet back from where it was, nothing but solid
rock would have formed its walls.

Sometimes, it takes only inches for success.

A piece of iron pipe provided me with a weapon of sorts,
and then I went out into the corridor. The aborigines
guarding the storeroom spotted me immediately. I'd gotten twisted around and hadn't figured out the relative locations of the rooms. I thought I went away from the hallway
with the guards; I went into it.

I squared my shoulders and planted my feet, readying
for the attack. It never came. I frowned, wondering what
held the two men back. I was taller, stronger, more determined, but they had their spears and spear throwers. With
those, even in this enclosed space, they had the advantage
over me. And they didn't attack.

The two mumbled back and forth, casting occasional
glances in my direction. Then, as if I didn't exist, they
leaned back against the cold stone wall and started rolling a
cigarette. They didn't bother raising an alarm or even trying to corner me. Instead, the cigarette they passed back
and forth occupied their full attention.

But I had to find out why they ignored me. I walked over
to them and stopped. They glanced up but did nothing
more.

"What you blackfellas doing?" I asked.

"Watching," said the one on the right.

"What?" I asked.

"*Kutjara* prisoners. Inside." He tapped the wooden door
to the storage room.

Daniela's voice came through, mumbled but still distinct

enough to make out. "He said he's guarding two prisoners."

The other aborigine rattled off a thickly accented stream of Pitjandjara, none of which I understood. Again came Daniela's translation.

"He wants to know if the boy-child born to his wife is his."

I remembered what Daniela had told me earlier about the bushmen. They fell asleep and if they dreamed that a newborn was theirs, then it was. Otherwise, the child remained fatherless until some man claimed it. If no one did, the mother killed the infant as not possessing a soul pulled in from Dreamtime.

I thought that over for a second, then everything clicked into place.

I nodded vigorously, saying, "Blackfella proper big father." I tapped him on the chest. His answering smile told me he'd just accepted the responsibility of parenthood.

"What's happening, Nick?" came Daniela's disembodied voice. "Why are you talking with them? I don't understand."

"I think I do. Since no one can escape from the room, they know I'm not the same person as inside. Since I look like the man they put into the room—and they don't see anyway I could've escaped—I have to be a ghost."

"*That's* why he asked you if the boy was his!" exclaimed Daniela. "He thinks you're a ghost and inhabit the Dreaming, therefore you know all that sort of thing."

"Let's see how far this omnipotence goes," I said. Facing the abos, I boldly commanded, "Let Debbil Daniela out."

They frowned, as if pondering the fate of the world. I understood their dilemma. Whatever hold Marston had over them was strong, yet it wasn't as strong as a request from their Dreaming. I was a phantasm, a ghost, and claimed a special spot in their day-to-day lives.

Finally, the one holding the cigarette signalled to the other one. It might have been a request to finish off the smoke, but it wasn't. The man on the left unbolted the door.

"Daniela, come on out," I said. "And you, you there—
stay back!"

This charade satisfied the aborigines that my other self,
the real world self, remained in the storage room. After all,
the Dreaming self had ordered it. Therefore, it had to be.

"You plenny good fellas," I said. Both men smiled and
nodded. "You stay here and guard the door." Again the
nods.

"Nick, let's get out of here," implored Daniela. "This is
bloody frightening."

"I agree. If we get back to the radio shed, I can call in the
cavalry and be done with this entire radar station."

TWENTY-FIVE

"We're trapped, Nick! We can't get out that way. Too bloody many of those buggers." Daniela looked around, swiveling at the hips as if her feet had been pinned to the ground and was doomed to spend the rest of eternity fixed to this spot.

I grabbed her arm and pulled her toward the storeroom I'd first hidden the Russian sergeant in. The man had long since been rescued, leaving the room empty. We squeezed through the door at the same time and pulled it closed until only a narrow crack remained. I peered through it. The knot of people coming down the spiral ramp had been speaking fluent Russian.

I recognized one of the voices.

The small entourage stopped outside the door. I started to push the door all the way shut, then decided against it. Any slight movement might attract their attention. Especially Colonel Vladen Rokarov, head of special projects, Asian Directorate, KGB.

Rokarov and I had locked horns once before, and he'd come out second best. I was sure my face was permanently engraved on the man's mind. He had been dealing heroin through Hong Kong into Japan and Korea, heroin destined primarily for U.S. servicemen. The idea had been simple: hook enough soldiers on the drug and impair their usefulness.

It had been working well, too, because the Soviet financed the operation totally. Cheap opium came from the Golden Triangle in Laos and Cambodia, now virtually a new Soviet state. They refined the junk in Ho Chi Minh City, then smuggled it into Hong Kong on Czech freighters. From there, Vladen Rokarov personally saw that the smack made its way into the hands of KGB agents in Tokyo and Seoul.

I'd worked three months to infiltrate the fireworks company Rokarov used as a front in Hong Kong. Not only had I burned down the warehouse containing over five hundred kilos of smack, I'd removed his operatives in Tokyo and Seoul for good measure. We'd faced each other right at the end of the mission, almost like an old-time duel.

Each of us had a knife and our wits, nothing more. Colonel Rokarov had been both lucky and unlucky. My knife opened a gash in his chest starting over his appendix and running up to his left shoulder. It'd been bloody and there hadn't been anyway he could have lived—normally. He'd fallen off the roof of the warehouse. I torched the building, destroying its deadly cargo within and had counted Rokarov as dead.

He'd fallen into the back of a truck laden with silk kimonos. Those had broken his fall sufficiently to allow him to bribe the driver to take him to a safe house run by the KGB across the harbor in Kowloon. Vladen Rokarov had lived, but he carried the permanent mark of Killmaster on his body.

No, Rokarov wouldn't forget me, not in a hundred lifetimes.

My finger twitched in reflex action, wishing it curled around Wilhelmina's trigger. But both Luger and stiletto were still in captivity.

"Nick," whispered Daniela behind me, "what's happening? Are they going to catch us?"

"No," I said softly. "They're having a little meeting out in the hall. Quiet. Let me listen."

Ram Marston joined the Soviet officers. This made the spying even more pertinent.

"I see no bloody reason for you to make the trip, colonel," said Marston in his deep, booming voice.

"I thought to check up on this installation, nothing more," said the KGB officer. "The reports received in my office in Ho Chi Minh City indicate you are experiencing some extreme problems."

"No problems."

"There was an AXE agent here." The statement came out with a biting edge to it.

"I took care of him. We got him and a lady professor bottled up in a storeroom."

"I see," said Rokarov, as if considering every angle. "And this man is Nick Carter, agent N3?"

"I don't know anything about his code name, but he claimed to be Nick Carter." The gusto with which Marston spoke told me he'd learned of my brief dalliance with his daughter. If Marston had the chance, he'd kill me out of hand, not only for the danger I presented to subleasing part of his sheep ranch to the Russians, but also because I violated his ideas of propriety and moral behavior.

"How'd he get here?" asked Daniela, peering around my shoulder. I motioned her to silence.

"This," said Rokarov, "hardly seems likely, given that AXE agents are most capable, and this one in particular is their top field operative. I believe he has used you for his own purposes, Marston. He has allowed himself to be captured."

"For what reason?"

"That I do not know. Perhaps he wanted to be in the middle of this complex. Given the run of the station . . ."

"He's not got the run of the bloody station," snapped Marston. "The bloody submarine trip from Vietnam's addled your brains."

"I'm used to such travel. And the journey in that low-flying plane of yours from Groote likewise did not inflict any mental damage. No, Marston, you've been used as a pawn in Carter's game. He's too smart to be held for long. I know."

I have to admit feeling a moment's glow of pride. You're known by your enemies—Vladen Rokarov was one of the most wanted in AXE files. To have him crediting me with more intelligence than I'd shown thus far gave me a boost to the ego.

What would give me an even bigger share of pride of accomplishment would be to not only eliminate the radar station but Vladen Rokarov along with it.

"Come along then, colonel," said Marston, "and I'll show you how bloody smart this spy of yours is. I'll show you Mr. Nick Carter, all penned up neat as you please."

"I'd like to see that very much," said Rokarov in a voice designed to drop even searing desert temperatures several degrees.

The small group walked away, heading for the room where the two bushmen still smoked, perhaps the one congratulating the other on the birth of a son, and guarded an empty room. I opened the door and pulled Daniela along behind me.

"To the surface. Now." I shoved her toward the ramp.

"Not without you, Nick. You can't do anything against them. Not unarmed."

"I can try."

"I'm coming with you then, you complete and totally bloody fool."

"No!" I didn't want the woman along. Taking care of myself proved difficult enough at times. Having to watch after her, too, would detract from my efficiency. And I felt I needed all the skill and determination and concentration possible to blow up this radar unit and kill Vladen Rokarov.

The first seemed almost ludicrously easy to me compared with the second. The KGB colonel was a worthy opponent.

"I won't go alone to the surface, Nick."

The set of her mouth told me Daniela Rhys-Smith meant what she said. She had an iron core to her that wouldn't allow her to give in. Back in the storeroom she'd been frightened. I knew that she had to try and redeem herself in my eyes. No matter that things had looked bleak and that there wasn't anyway everyone can be strong all the time. She was a professor, dropped into the middle of a cauldron of espionage. This transcended her normal experience and expertise.

But she had shown weakness. Now she thought bravado would make her courage whole again.

I glanced down the corridor in the direction Marston and Rokarov had taken, then back at Daniela. There wasn't any way to retreat and attack at the same time. The thought flashed through my mind that a quick blow to Daniela's temple would knock her out, leaving me free to pursue the completion of my mission.

Then I discarded that.

"Back," I ordered. "Up to the surface. I've got to report in to my backup in Sydney and get the troops in here. And then I can find a weapon."

With luck, I'd have this snake's nest cleaned out before the heavy artillery came in.

TWENTY-SIX

"They'll catch us, Nick!" Daniela gripped hard at my arm as she pointed toward the rock outcropping concealing the entrance to the underground radar station. Four aborigines silently filed out of the hidden doorway, seemingly appearing from thin air. All carried spears and knives.

"Quiet," I said. Thinking hard, I wondered what to do next. Vladen Rokarov had found out about our escape too quickly. I'd hoped to have a good half hour start when I'd gotten Daniela out of the storeroom. That lead had been cut to minutes when the KGB colonel came onto the scene. Still, I had to count myself as lucky.

If I'd been in the room when Rokarov walked in, I would have been dead five seconds later. Vladen Rokarov didn't forget old enemies; he eliminated them. What small head start we had had to be used intelligently.

"What are we going to do, Nick?" the woman demanded. "Those men are *good* trackers. They exist by being able to track across stone, over the desert, by—"

"Shut up!" I said, too loud. The four abos heard and stopped, ears cocked and waiting for another sound to give away our hiding spot. I crouched down further behind the small boulder and worked out the few alternatives we had.

"What are you waiting for?" came a voice I knew all too well. Rokarov had emerged from the underground station to personally conduct the search. Marston might screw up. Vladen Rokarov wouldn't.

The aborigines cackled among themselves like hens roosting, then one of them said, "Ghosts."

"What?" The bellow from the KGB colonel rolled through the night. "What do you mean, 'ghosts?' That's ridiculous. Where are Carter and the woman?"

"Uh, colonel," came Marston's somewhat subdued voice.

I figured he'd been put in his place in a hurry when he couldn't produce the infamous agent N3 of AXE. Even an unassuming university professor—and a woman, at that— had escaped his clutches. Ram Marston was fortunate to be alive. Rokarov didn't appreciate ineptness, or allow the incompetent to live long.

"What?" Brusque, the Russian officer felt he had other things to cope with beyond blundering Australian ranchers.

"The abos, they're saying that Carter and Rhys-Smith are ghosts."

"I know that, you fool!"

"Ghosts mean something different to them. It . . . it's not superstition with them."

"There are no ghosts, comrade," said Rokarov in a low, deadly voice. The tone wasn't lost on Marston. I imagined he turned a shade paler, even if it wasn't possible to see from where Daniela and I hid.

"It's part of their religion. Carter's convinced them he's not of this world, that he belongs in the Dreaming."

The silence from Rokarov hung heavily. Marston rattled on, trying to cure his own nervousness with speech.

"They think he walked through walls down there, and that makes him a ghost from the Dreaming. They won't help us track them down because it violates their . . ."

Four shots rang out. I half rose to attack. Only Daniela's hand on my shoulder kept me from taking Rokarov on with my bare hands. He'd cold-bloodedly murdered the four aborigines with him because they had adopted a view counter to his. As a Soviet soldier and high-ranking member of the Communist Party, he had to officially and publicly disavow all religions, but this went deeper.

No one crossed Vladen Rokarov. He couldn't have cared less about the aborigines' views. He'd killed them simply because Marston had said they wouldn't obey and come hunting us. The reasons were incidental.

"Colonel," said Marston in a choked tone, "we're in for bloody rough times if Pierce ever finds out you've snuffed four of his men. That one's his brother."

"This Pierce, he is a leader of the savages?"

"Yes."

"Tell him that his 'ghost' killed these men. Tell him that the 'ghosts' are dangerous to him and his tribe. If that does not work, then kill him."

"I . . . Colonel, please!"

"Do it. Or I shall see to your removal."

Vladen Rokarov spun and vanished back into the shadowy underground. Marston stood alone, visibly shaking. I pulled Daniela away, heading in the direction of Pierce's camp.

When we were far enough away that Marston was out of earshot, I said, "We've got to enlist the aid of the abos. It's the only way we're going to stay alive. Get to them first, explain what's happened and maybe they'll help us."

"Nick, it doesn't work that way with the bushmen. Pierce might be put out about his brother being killed—the others were related distantly to him, too—but he won't do anything. Their familial ties are . . . different. It's not that he doesn't care; it's just that their minds work on a different level."

"How can we get him to help us?"

Daniela shrugged and looked miserable. "He might decide it's none of his business. If he does that, there's no amount of arguing that will change his mind before Marston tracks us down."

"Let's both go. We've got to give it a try."

I felt what little edge we had evaporating. Trying to reach Marston's radio transmitter was out of the question. The very first thing Rokarov would do was place sentries over the shed, and those men would be his own Russian soldiers. While the technicians manning the radar station weren't front line combat soldiers, fear of Rokarov would lend them abilities equal to the finest the Soviets had anywhere in the world.

Getting to Pierce ahead of the KGB colonel gave us the only escape route we could take.

"Run, Daniela, run!" I urged. "We've got to make it to Pierce's camp before they do."

The cold night air lanced through my lungs as I set the pace. The bugs had gone to sleep for the night, a small boon but a welcome one. Several times Daniela stumbled and fell, but she valiantly kept up until we saw the dozen campfires blazing around Pierce's camp.

"There's the *ngura,*" gasped out Daniela. "Please, Nick, let me catch my breath."

"In the camp." I almost carried her the rest of the way. I spotted Pierce squatting beside a fire near the middle of the encampment. He roasted a haunch of wombat, one of his favorite meals. That might put the man into a good mood.

I could only hope.

"Pierce," called out Daniela. "Plenny good *mako.*"

"Plenny," he agreed, rubbing his stomach.

"Don't talk about his damn food," I said, jerking the woman impatiently. "Get to the point." I looked around the perimeter of the camp, hunting for any sign that the Russians had arrived ahead of us. I saw nothing.

"These talks can't be rushed. If they are, he'll feel we're violating tribal mores."

"We wouldn't want that," I said sarcastically.

"He'll kill us if we do."

"Get on with it."

Daniela talked on and on in the Pitjandjara dialect. I made out certain words taken from English, but the general drift of the conversation eluded me. What I saw instantly was the ripple of interest starting at the far side of the camp. Strangers came in. And that meant Rokarov.

Daniela saw, too. She pointed toward Pierce's shelter made from brush.

"The *wiltja,* Nick, we can hide there."

We dived for cover just as fire light reflected off Rokarov's highly polished knee-high boots. The KGB colonel strode into the illumination cast by the fire. Pierce only glanced up at him, then went back to eating the wombat.

"*This* is their leader?" Rokarov asked, contempt in his voice.

"Please, colonel, let me handle this," begged Marston. I knew how much the Australian station owner was backed into a corner. I'd never have thought the man capable of groveling like he did now. Rokarov held the whip hand. Not only did he control Marston's future concerning the sheep station, he also held power over Marston through the man's daughter. I felt a slight trembling as I considered what Rokarov might do to Claire if Marston disobeyed the smallest of orders.

For what seemed a lifetime, Daniela and I hunkered in the drafty brush hut while the KGB colonel and Marston interrogated Pierce.

"Colonel Rokarov, he's getting restless," Marston finally said. He nervously glanced around the camp. The bushmen had circled the pair. Even with a pair of automatics, Rokarov and Marston stood no chance against ten spearmen.

I longed to call out that Rokarov had killed four of their number, but I refrained. My hands weren't any less bloody on that score.

"They're going, Nick. We *did* it." I felt Daniela's relief almost as much as I did my own. "I managed to convince Pierce that we needed time to enter the Dreaming. That's considered inviolate among the Pitjandjara. But I don't know what he's going to do now. That Russian colonel made some pretty dire threats. Marston might just carry them out."

"We've got a few hours," I told her. "That'll have to be enough." But even as I said it, I wondered exactly how much time we did have. The first light of dawn brightened the eastern sky. I'd lost all track of time and had thought Pierce and the others were eating dinner, not breakfast. With the bright light of day came easier aerial surveillance by Marston's two planes.

Whatever I did had to be done fast.

TWENTY-SEVEN

I took cover the instant I heard the airplane engine. Less than ten seconds later, it roared overhead. My hands longed for the hard, metallic feel of a gun. Mentally sighting on the plane, I followed it across the sky until it vanished behind a hill less than a mile to the south. Both of Marston's planes had been continually aloft since sunup, harassing and badgering me in my attempts to get to the house. I didn't know what I'd do once I got there, but it'd have to be a better place to start than the abo camp.

The most modern weapon Pierce had was a battered 1903 Enfield rifle. Somewhere in all the shuffle, his Smith & Wesson Police Positive had been lost and none of the other weapons in his camp had ammunition. Daniela had bartered at length trying to get the aborigine to loan me his rifle—his *riple*—and she'd failed. The man would sooner give me his first two wives than let the rifle out of his sight.

Daniela had remained in camp while I tried to get to Marston's. That had been a major battle won for my side. Not having to look after her while I darted in and out between Rokarov's patrols gave me added mobility, though that maneuverability hadn't amounted to much yet.

It would. It had to.

I waited as a pair of Russian soldiers stalked along, muttering between themselves. I gripped the only weapon Pierce would loan me, wondering if it would work. The boomerang had been used hard and long. The ironwood had nicks knocked out of its cutting edge, and blood from numerous kills stained the sides. Pierce had given me one single lesson in throwing. Watching him do it made it look easy. I wasn't so sure, but the time had come to try it out.

I rose, aimed, prayed and let fly.

The wooden crescent tumbled end over end, then began the slow curve back to me. I'd missed both soldiers by a long ways. But not only did the boomerang return, neither soldier noticed its passage. I had another chance. Snaring the boomerang at shoulder level, I brought back my arm, aimed again and let loose.

The single grunt of pain from the Russian in the lead rewarded my efforts. He sank to his knees, hands fluttering to the cut on the side of his head. His comrade simply stared, not knowing what had happened. This gave me the seconds needed to rush across the intervening distance and make a desperate dive. My arms circled the soldier's legs, tightened, pulled him down.

"You!" he cried in Russian, even as he fought. The man was young, strong, lithe. He wiggled and turned and kicked and almost escaped. My advantages were surprise and experience.

He died, my arm circling his throat. I tightened up even more when I felt him go limp. I doubted if he faked death as an old pro might, but I had to be sure. The choke hold released after another minute, I eased him to the ground.

"At least I'll have some modern weapons," I said to myself, reaching over for the man's AK-47. It was a bulky, clumsy, noisy rifle but virtually indestructible. It had few working parts and could be dragged through mud and sand and water and any other combat situation without unduly affecting it. My hand had just touched the barrel when a hasty *pwing!* sounded.

Pain lanced up my arm from the splintering bullet striking the receiver of the AK-47 I'd reached for. I collapsed, then rolled and kept rolling—without the gun. Some other patrol had seen me and opened fire. I cursed my bad timing. Another few seconds and I would have been armed with a rifle.

"Give it up, Carter," came the loud command. I recognized Marston's voice immediately. "I don't have any grudge against you, cobber. Just come on out and let's talk this over, man to man."

I didn't answer. To do so would be to give away my position. Mobility. That was the only asset I had. It had to be used to the utmost now or I'd die. Again I silently cursed losing the AK-47. With it, I'd turn the tables in a hurry. Marston would be my prey. As long as he held me at a distance with his rifle, he remained the predator.

Going down a sandy gulch at a quick clip, I almost fell over an abo sitting and patiently working at chipping a flint knife. He glanced up, then dismissed me as unimportant and went back to his work.

"Whitefella need help," I said earnestly. "Friend of Pierce. Relative of Mickey. You related?" That finally got his attention. I worried that Marston might push his hunt too fast for me to make good contact with this warrior. Dealing with Stone Age people is difficult at the best of times.

I found it almost impossible to contain my haste now. I wondered who was the more civilized.

"Sister married to Mickey's cousin Jimmy," the abo said. We continued comparing family trees until he seemed satisfied I wasn't just any stranger blundering along out in the desert.

"Nice knife," I complimented, looking at the wicked edge he chipped onto the flint. He shrugged. "Nice spear, too. Can I try it?"

We haggled for another minute before he gave me both his spear and spear thrower. I had the impression he did it to get rid of me as much as anything else. I'd interrupted "proper big business" and had set back his work by some minutes.

Hefting the *woomera,* I wondered if it was as easy to use as it looked. The spear thrower added power to the forward thrust. The spear itself was heavy, hard and virtually indestructible.

A crunch of sand. I twisted, drew back and sent the spear

hurling forward. The muscles in my upper arm and shoulder screamed in protest, but the spear flew straight and true.

The Russian soldier gasped, clutched at the wooden stalk blossoming from his chest, then fell heavily, the thirsty desert sands drinking his blood as it slowly drained from his lifeless body. I ran forward, wondering at the kill. Marston had been the one hot on my trail. Had another Soviet soldier blundered onto the track or had Marston sent this one on ahead?

It didn't matter one way or the other. I now had a rifle. I picked up the man's AK-47, then stopped. I felt a stirring, a familiar presence. On impulse, I dropped to my knees and began searching the dead man. What I found brightened my outlook immensely.

He carried both Wilhelmina and Hugo. I guessed he'd killed the abo who'd gotten my weapons—or he'd found them on one of the dead bodies created by Vladen Rokarov in his mini-slaughter. Either way, I felt whole again.

My stiletto slipped between belt and pants in the small of my back. I carried Wilhelmina. Before I left the dead soldier, I pulled the spear from his chest and retrieved the spear thrower. Retracing my steps, I found the aborigine still patiently chipping at his new primitive Stone Age artifact.

"Here're your weapons back," I told him. "They work good."

"Course, you bloody stupid whitefella," he said, without even looking up. He never questioned the fresh blood. Death was part and parcel of his life in the Outback.

I struggled through shifting sand until I made the top of a large sand dune. Peering around in the increasingly hot desert proved difficult. Heat shimmer caused the landscape to shift and shake as if seen through the side of an aquarium filled with turbulent water. But enough came through to make me smile.

I spotted Rokarov and two men with him not a hundred yards away. And they hadn't yet seen me. I retreated behind the crest of the dune and worked my way around to their rear. Less than twenty yards away, I heard Rokarov complaining.

"You've been in this desert for months. What do you mean you can't find him?"

"But, Colonel Rokarov," complained one, "we are radar technicians, not foot soldiers."

"Even foot soldiers would have troubles here," said the second man. "This heat is killing us."

"If you do not find Carter immediately, you need not worry about the heat. I will kill you." He drew the small 7.63mm automatic from his holster and pointed it directly at the second soldier.

I took aim and fired. The soldier jerked and fell, dead.

The KGB colonel's expression helped give me a feeling of repaying him. And my opportune and accurate shot had instilled enough fear in the other soldier to make him act. He thought the colonel had murdered his friend.

The barrel of the assault rifle rose. I waited for the ironic and poetically justified end to come to the KGB officer.

Vladen Rokarov is one of the Soviets' best, and he showed it now. He recovered in time to stoop, toss up a shower of blinding sand and fire his own weapon first. He kept firing until I heard the slide on the automatic lock open. He was out of ammo.

"Having trouble, Vladen?" I called out, standing. Wilhelmina came down slowly to form a perfect sight picture on the Russian colonel's chest.

"Carter!" he cried. "I might have known. You made me kill my own man."

"Nonsense, colonel. I'd really hoped he'd kill you. I had no quarrel with him. He's nothing more than a simple radar technician out of his league."

"Out of his league," said Rokarov. "Such quaint idioms you Americans use."

"Goodbye, colonel," I said, my finger squeezing smoothly on the Luger's trigger.

TWENTY-EIGHT

My reflexes took over from common sense when I heard movement behind me. I spun, dropped and fired in one swift, smooth movement. The abo who'd been so busily chipping his flint knife died without a sound. I jerked back to face Rokarov but was too late. The wily KGB colonel had taken the opportunity to get out of my line of fire.

I was torn between checking the fallen aborigine and going after Rokarov. I chose the latter. The man should never have come up behind me like that. He'd probably heard the conversation and came to see what the "ghosts" discussed. To him it probably amounted more to curiosity about his religion than an overt attempt to snoop.

After all, Daniela had worked hard to convince Pierce and the others that we were creatures from their Dreaming and not of this reality. The Russians had long since done it, apparently by accident rather than design. The way Rokarov treated the bushmen convinced me that the Soviets knew very little about the natives.

"Give it up, Rokarov," I called. "You're out of ammunition."

The faint click of a metallic catch closing told me I was wrong; he had another clip with him. I could count on at least eight rounds coming my way if I got careless, maybe more.

I'd stayed too long in one spot. Rokarov had gone up the far side of the sand dune and dropped flat on the summit. He sighted over the top. Four shots rang out causing sand to kick up around my feet. I danced like a cowboy in an old western, then dived behind a small boulder. Returning fire, I drove him out of sight.

But I'd gone through five shots of my own. And I didn't have another clip for Wilhelmina's hungry maw. My attention turned to the site where the two Russian soldiers lay. They had rifles. Both of them—or one with the other's ammo—would serve me well. If I got to them before Rokarov.

He was a pro, too, and hated the idea of leaving behind usable weapons and ammunition. We both knew that a protracted firefight required bullets. To get it meant risking much. With time and men on his side, I had to be the one to take the risks.

I weaved, dodged and ran as fast as I could to the nearest body. No leaden rain greeted me. I jerked free the AK-47 from under the fallen soldier, then hefted it up just as Rokarov made his presence known. He had continued circling until he was behind me. He even used the same boulder I had used for cover earlier.

Whether he was lucky, a damn good shot, or both, I'll never know. His slug ripped the rifle from my hands. I took in the scene with a swift glance. The rifle was useless. Using the soldier's body as a barricade, I scooted around and found the other man's AK-47.

"Give it up, Rokarov," I shouted. "I've got the firepower now." To let him know, I sent a few rounds smashing into the rock. The boulder began crumbling under the onslaught. I loosened another burst and shards of rock flew in all directions. Under this cover, I rose and ran forward. If Vladen Rokarov dared show himself, I'd cut him in two with a dozen heavy slugs from his own country's chief export weapon.

I stood atop the rock, rifle aimed down at . . . nothing.

"What's wrong, Carter?" came his mocking words from some distance. In the desert terrain, with its rocky gulches and miniature canyons I couldn't be sure where he was. Maybe close, maybe some distance away. "Aren't you pleased at my escape?"

"Why should I be happy about it?"

"This is the confrontation we've both wanted ever since Hong Kong."

"You've wanted it, Rokarov. Until six months ago, we thought you were dead."

"You thought you'd killed me, Carter," he said. "Until the assassination of the American undersecretary in Korea, you thought you'd killed me. I'm stronger than any U.S. agent. Anyone, do you hear! Especially you!"

Others might have been duped into thinking Rokarov had gone out of control, that he bragged too much. I knew his psychological profile well. He tried to gull me into thinking he'd gone off the deep end. I might underestimate him if I thought him crazy.

The last thing in the world I wanted to do was miscalculate now. I had to treat him for what he was: one of the most dangerous men in the KGB. And I had to show him what I was: the most dangerous man in the U.S. secret service.

All the time I'd spent in the desert, struggling out on the Nullarbor Plain after the airplane crash, the time driving through the spinifex and talking with Pierce and his tribe, came to my aid now. I knew what to avoid, what to do. I counted on Rokarov being familiar with jungles, not desert. He'd spent most of the last ten years in Southeast Asia and the Orient. This was the only clear advantage I saw over him.

The man was dangerous.

Lugging along the captured AK-47, I made my way up one rocky arroyo. Once, I saw a flash of movement. My finger tightened and a half dozen rounds surged from the barrel of the rifle. A snake exploded into bloody bits. I moved closer and poked at the taipan. Shuddering, I counted the bullets as well spent. This was one of the most poisonous snakes in all Australia.

"Getting nervous, Carter? Shooting at shadows?" came the taunting voice. Rokarov had changed his tact. Seeing I wouldn't buy him going around the bend, he tried to anger me. "You're really not very good at this sort of thing."

"What comes next, Rokarov? Do you try to buy me? Make me an offer. I want to hear what the KGB thinks I'm worth."

"You? Worth?" He laughed.

Fire seared my upper arm. Blood spurted from the bullet wound and showered me with a red rain. I let the AK-47 fall, as if he'd fatally wounded me. The hardest part of the charade came when I found I'd fallen onto some of the bayonet-bladed spinifex. A barbed leaf thrust up into my side, giving me worse pain than the bullet wound. Poisons slowly trickled into my system, burning abominably.

I didn't move, even from the spinifex. Or the bugs crawling over me. Or the trickling blood from my arm. The coagulation over the shallow bullet track would keep me from bleeding to death—I wasn't too badly hurt.

But as I lay deathly still, my hand held Wilhelmina in an easy grip. All Rokarov had to do was present me with one clean shot and his career would come to an end.

"Do stand up, Carter, and let me have another shot at you. I know you're not that badly hurt, though you do seem to be impaled on that damnable grass."

I knew he didn't see me. If he had, there would have been a followup bullet. I hated leaving behind the AK-47, but if Rokarov lurked behind a clump of bushes where I thought he did, he had a good view of the rifle. Let it stay as bait. Pulling myself painfully free of the spinifex, I cautiously checked my wounds as I hid behind a rocky embankment. Nothing serious. Binding my arm kept it from doing more than oozing blood. The spinifex puncture had to wait until I was done with Vladen Rokarov.

Crawling on my belly brought me to a rocky overlook that should have given me an unimpeded shot at him.

He'd moved.

Sand kicked up all around as he opened fire. Rokarov hadn't been taken in for an instant by my leaving the rifle in plain sight. He'd moved, positioned himself and still had the high ground.

"The radar station is lost, Rokarov," I called out, working myself behind a rock. "Give it up and go home."

"Go home? You're changing your tune, Carter. Now you're willing to let me walk away. I don't believe it."

"Why not? We'll have other chances at one another."

Even as I spoke, I saw the opening. And so did Rokarov. We each started firing. My Luger fired twice before the toggles locked back, the clip empty. Rokarov got off one shot more before he exhausted his ammunition.

"What now, Carter? Hand to hand?"

"Why not?" I said, rising. I reached behind and found Hugo. The stiletto gleamed brightly in the hot desert sun.

Rokarov also stood. A British leaf-bladed commando knife appeared in his hand.

"See what you did before, Carter?" the KGB colonel ripped open his khaki uniform blouse. An ugly white scar crossed his chest, starting just above his navel and ending over his left nipple. "For this I will gut you!"

We approached one another slowly. The heat took its toll on our strength, even as the cat and mouse hunting through the ravines had. Circling, testing each other's balance and reach, we feinted, tried all the preliminary attacks necessary to set up the kill.

It came in a rush. For a heat stopping instant, I wasn't sure if I'd killed Rokarov or he'd killed me. Then I knew. We'd both scored the other. Rivers of blood covered our bodies, mingled and made us blood brothers.

Or brothers in blood. Rokarov wasn't that different from me, not in the way he carried out his assignments. Ruthlessness we both had. If a single difference existed between us, it was my conscience. I often regretted the killing I had to do. I regretted killing Mickey and the flint-chipping abo. One had been self-defense, the other an unfortunate death, but I regretted both.

Rokarov would never have thought of either man after killing them.

Straining, striving, we fought locked together on the barren, rocky rise in the Australian Outback. We fought until I heard a booming bass voice I knew all too well cry out, "Stop it, Carter. Stop it or I kill her!"

Ram Marston held a gun to Daniela's head.

I released Rokarov and pushed him back, dropping my hands to my side to signify defeat.

TWENTY-NINE

"No, you fool, don't try it!" screamed Rokarov. He was a professional; he knew what was going to happen.

As my hand came down, making Marston think I'd given in to his demands, my knife lightly flipped over so that I held it by the blade tip. A quick wrist motion sent the knife spinning through the air, a flashing, cartwheeling messenger of death. My aim was off slightly, and the needlepoint struck Marston high on the right cheek rather than through his right eye.

It was enough.

The man howled in pain and reached for the wound. Daniela kicked backward, striking him on the shins. The pain confused him, Daniela got away and I stood in front of him. It hardly mattered that he still had a pistol and I had only my bare hands. A quick kick disarmed him. A spinning kick to his stomach knocked him to the ground.

"Nick!" called Daniela. She tossed Hugo back to me. The knife hadn't gone too far afield after it slashed open Marston's cheek.

"Carter, no, you can't. I wouldn't have killed her. I wouldn't!"

The man's pleading made me sick. I lunged and the stiletto easily slipped into the man's heart. He died without uttering another sound.

"Nick, oh God, Nick!" cried Daniela. She clung to me.

I roughly shoved her away, pivoting to face Vladen Rokarov. I didn't know why he'd left me alone to kill

Marston. He should have attacked the instant my attention was diverted.

The KGB colonel had vanished.

I relaxed a little. I'd tracked him down once and could do it again.

"Sorry, Daniela," I apologized. "Business first." I held her shaking body until the worst of the sobs had passed. "Rokarov escaped. I have to go get him."

"H-he caught me while I was hiding in Pierce's camp," Daniela stuttered.

"Rokarov?"

"No, Marston!" She looked up at me as if I were stupid. "Pierce and the others went to hunt, and Marston found me. I think he knew we were both there earlier, but hadn't told the Russian officer."

That made sense. The way Rokarov intimidated the rancher made Marston all the more likely to grandstand to regain favor. He thought capturing Daniela and then using her as a lever against me would let him bask in the sunny light of Rokarov's approval.

He obviously didn't know Vladen Rokarov very well. The only acceptable job to him is one done perfectly. Anything less is subject to punishment in his KGB Directorate. Marston had already screwed up too many times to be allowed to live. I had no idea what Rokarov planned, but letting Ram Marston continue running the station as he had wasn't in the cards.

"So Marston brought you out here, saw Rokarov and me fighting, then used you as extortion bait?"

She nodded, her brown hair flying in wild disarray around her face. Her eyes widened: for the first time Daniela Rhys-Smith figured out how deadly this game actually was. Before, being imprisoned and threatened, had been frightening but nothing actually that dangerous. Not realizing it showed her innocence in such things. Now that Marston had dragged her from Pierce's camp, shoved the gun to her head—and she'd watched a man die—Daniela had come around to real understanding. And she didn't like it one bit.

"You're a cold-blooded man, aren't you, Nick?"

"It helps."

"And they're even worse."

"I hope I'm better, but whatever goes down, I have to be smarter and more dangerous to stay alive."

She squared her shoulders and took a half step back. "Let me help. I want to help you find the Russian."

I shook my head sadly. Daniela hadn't learned anything, after all. While she might realize this wasn't a Sunday afternoon parlor game, she hadn't had the deadly lesson drummed into her head that Rokarov would kill her and never notice the strain.

"This is my job, just like finding out about the aborigines is yours. You do yours well, I do mine well. You'd laugh at my attempts to interview Pierce, wouldn't you?"

"Yes."

"You'd die trying to do my job."

"You saved my life, Nick. I want to help."

"Then get the hell out of my way." Standing arguing with the woman let Rokarov get an even larger head start. I figured he circled around to get back to the radar station. Before it had been a personal vendetta with him. Now that Marston had died and others of his small command were removed, he had to salvage as much of the operation as he could.

That meant getting to a radio and contacting a trawler or submarine for reinforcements.

I didn't feel any driving urgency to find him because it would take so long for those backups to arrive. If he radioed the sub that had dropped him off on the northern coast near Groote, he'd have to wait a day or longer for them to arrive. I doubted any Soviet troops were closer. This had been a clandestine operation and, like all such efforts, required few men.

"We're going back to Marston's house."

"Claire!" gasped Daniela. "The Russian officer is going to nab her!"

"I doubt it. Rokarov doesn't think in those terms. If he used her at all, it would have been against Marston. He knows holding her wouldn't slow me down for an instant."

"It didn't slow you down when Marston held me, did it?"

Daniela finally realized the logic in my actions. Cold-blooded, maybe, but the only way to operate. She wasn't stupid, just uneducated in the ways of espionage. I saw by the expression on her face that she wanted to return to her ivory tower at the university. This wasn't her kind of action.

We hadn't gone ten feet when Daniela stooped down and picked up my Luger. She turned and silently handed it to me.

"Thanks," I said. As we walked, I cleaned out Wilhelmina's action, getting every bit of sand out of her workings. Lugers are precision instruments, totally reliable in combat but requiring extensive maintenance. The pistol would never jam on me because of the care lavished in times like this.

After twenty minutes hiking, we topped a hill overlooking the Marston station. To the far left sat the small radio shack. Both my and Marston's Land Rovers stood by the barn. No sign of life anywhere.

"The radio shack's where Rokarov headed," I told Daniela. "But I'd like to have some ammo. We'll have to make a detour to the house. I saw a box of 9mm shells in Marston's gun cabinet."

"I can get it, Nick."

Rokarov might have gone for the house. If so, Daniela would be going into the jaws of danger. But everything I knew about the KGB colonel pointed to him trying to save the radar site by radioing for aid.

"Go. And take Wilhelmina with you. Make sure that the shells you get fit into the chamber."

She was no stranger to firearms. She pulled back the toggles and examined the receiver.

"All right, Nick. I can do it."

"Bloody well hurry, then," I told her. She reached up and grabbed a handful of hair to pull my face to hers for a quick kiss, then she was off. I watched until she was in the house before starting for the radio shack. I don't know what I would have done if there had been shouts or shots at the house.

I put all that out of my mind and fixed my concentration

on Rokarov, on the radio shack, on capturing him.

I might have guessed wrong; I hadn't. Less than ten feet from the shed I heard the KGB man's voice uttering the gutteral syllables of a plea for aid in Russian. Kicking in the door interrupted him. I took advantage of him trying to turn and face me. I kicked the chair out from under him and spun the frequency dial.

Rokarov moved faster than any human I'd ever seen. He upended me with a football tackle that would have made Harvey Martin proud and kept on moving until he got out of the confines of the shed.

The colonel stood in the sun, gleaming as sweat ran down his naked torso. The scar I'd given him in Hong Kong blazed like a white sash across his chest.

"Come, Carter, come and let's be done with this once and for all." The knife he'd had earlier appeared as if by magic in his hand.

I said nothing as I gathered my feet under me and rose, Hugo between us. Rokarov and I circled, looking for the slightest of openings. We were both good, but a fight like this can't last over a few seconds. We knew all the tricks, all the tactics.

I was faster this time.

Rokarov lunged. I dropped Hugo in favor of a double-handed grip on the man's wrist. I turned, twisted and Rokarov's feet left the ground. For a long instant his entire body hung parallel to the ground at my shoulder level. Then he fell like a ton of bricks. I didn't follow him down— and I didn't release his wrist.

The loud snapping noise preceded the man's agonized scream by only a split second. I'd dislocated Rokarov's shoulder and broken his wrist.

Even better, I'd captured him alive.

He glared at me as I recovered my knife. His anger fed my feeling of accomplishment.

Vladen Rokarov was my prisoner and his radar station out of commission. That left only one piece of unfinished business.

I knew now why Hawk had sent me blind into this mission.

THIRTY

"Here, Nick," called out Daniela. She tossed me my Luger. The heft of the metallic butt in my hand made me feel good, even though Rokarov put up no further fight. He seemed reconciled to the idea that he was my prisoner and that he'd soon be on his way to Pacific AXE headquarters in Hawaii for interrogation.

I knew better. The man continually plotted how to turn the tables on me and make this into a coup for Russia and Vladen Rokarov.

"Thanks." I eyed the gun, wondering if I should make certain that Daniela had found 9mm shells properly fitting it. Then she gave me the high sign telling me that all was well. I hadn't heard any shots so she must have jacked several shells through the mechanism to make certain of the caliber.

"What now, Nick?"

"We call in the troops. I've eliminated most of the Russians working at the radar site, but there are a few left."

"Only four," said Daniela. "I heard Marston complaining about it."

Marston had no reason to lie in Daniela's hearing. He hadn't been a subtle person to lay such a trap. He'd meant it. Besides, Marston thought Daniela was permanently captured and ready to be killed. He wouldn't have watched what he said around her, another mark of the amateur.

"Let me call back to Sydney," I said, spinning the dials

to get the proper frequency. I kept an eye on Rokarov, but the man still made no overt move. Maybe he wanted to get out of the game after this fiasco for him. His superiors in Dzerzhinsky Square in Moscow might decide he needed retiring—permanently. I'd pass this thought along to Hawk, when I spoke to him.

Or maybe Vladen Rokarov waited for something else.

"Who are you calling?" asked Daniela.

"My backup on this. Ah, here's the reply." The static boomed from the speakers, but cutting through was Sanford Marian's nasal twang.

"I say, old boy, you didn't make it back on schedule. Is anything wrong?"

"Everything's fine, Marian. In fact, I want you to get out to Marston's station as soon as possible. I've got some nice baggage for you."

"Baggage?"

"Russian-made. Remember Hong Kong a while back? My good comrade Rokarov?"

"He's there?"

"Wanting to vacation in Hawaii, at our special spa."

"I say, you have been busy. I'll call up all our friends and—"

"No!"

"What's that, Carter? You *don't* want assistance?"

"Just you. I've had a thought about why Hawk sent me out blind like he did."

"Oh?"

"This station is a nice place. I think he wants this kept quiet so that we can . . . use it ourselves, without annoying guests dropping in all the time. Nice vacation spot, don't you agree?"

Marian laughed. I hoped my intended meaning came through to him. While I doubted we were being intercepted on this frequency, we had to play it like we might be. I had to get through to Marian that Hawk intended to use the radar station for continued surveillance of Australian launches—but the information would go to the U.S. instead of the Soviets.

"I understand perfectly. Bloody clever of him. I'll fly out by myself. See you by sundown."

"Be waiting for you," I said, clicking off the power. The hum from the huge thyratron in back died and the sole source of heat in the room now came from the blistering sun overhead. I pointed my gun at Rokarov and told him, "Back to the house. We're waiting for the cavalry to arrive."

Daniela pressed close by me all the way back.

"There's a small plane landing, Nick!" came Claire Marston's excited voice. "It must be whoever you've been waiting for."

I hadn't told her about her father's death—and neither had Daniela. I had Rokarov securely tied and gagged. While it might be crueler not telling her, I felt the right time hadn't come yet. It would. Soon. Maybe too soon.

"Let's go meet it," I suggested, after checking Rokarov one last time. With his broken wrist—I'd relocated his shoulder for him—he wasn't going to escape easily, not the way I had him trussed up. He could be left unguarded for a few minutes.

And he hadn't even tried to escape. I had him pegged as being docile for some time to come.

Daniela and I went out to the landing strip and watched the small Cessna taxi down and stop. The dust cloud obscured Marian as he got out, but I recognized him immediately from the way he walked. He'd come alone, as I'd suggested.

"Hello, old chap," he greeted me. "Well done, if I understood your message properly."

"You did. I've got Vladen Rokarov all ready for shipment to Pacific Sector headquarters. And the Russian radar station is limping along. Only four technicians left. They won't pose any problem for us."

"I should say not." He eyed Daniela suspiciously. "And this must be Dr. Rhys-Smith."

"How do you do," Daniela said coldly, reacting to his distrust.

"It's all right, Sanford. She knows all about the unit. In fact, Daniela helped quite a bit. Right in the middle of things." We approached the house. Claire Marston came to the door to greet us.

"And I believe you know Claire," I told Marian, slowing so that I'd be a half step behind him.

The expression on Claire's face told the story. She looked startled, then happy, then frightened in a cavalcade of emotion.

"Sanford!" she screamed, as the man ducked, dodged and grabbed her. He spun her around, a small pistol pressed into her side.

Facing the same situation twice in one day prepared me for action. Even as Sanford Marian darted forward, I was drawing my Luger. As he turned, I aimed and fired. The heavy 9mm slug smashed into his shoulder and threw him into the house, through the open door.

"Out of my way!" I shouted. But Claire had collapsed to her knees and got in my way. Marian slammed and locked the door. I had to break the window next to the door to get another shot at him. I fired and hit him again, but the wound couldn't have been more than annoying. I'd failed to make a clean kill.

"Nick, I don't understand," said Daniela in a shocked voice. "I thought he was on our side. And Claire. . . ."

"Tend to her. She's had a bad shock. Her lover's just tried to kill her."

I didn't hear any more of Daniela's pleas for information. I had to find and kill Sanford Marian.

No traitorous agent in AXE can be allowed to live.

THIRTY-ONE

I stopped to check Rokarov's bonds. He remained securely tied, but his demeanor had changed. He realized that, for him, the "cavalry" had come and had failed in its rescue. He fought violently against the ropes, but his broken wrist impeded any real progress in freeing himself. I left him tied to the chair in what had once been my bedroom.

Tracking down Sanford Marian proved easier than I'd hoped. A trail of blood led directly to the barn. I approached cautiously, wary of an ambush. Wounded, an animal becomes even more dangerous, and Marian was one of the most deadly in our espionage jungle.

Two shots rang out. I dived and took cover behind a bale of hay used to feed the horses. I didn't stay here long enough to get comfortable. I ran toward the barn's open door and ducked into the dank coolness, turning immediately from the light to avoid being silhouetted. Horses neighed and kicked against their stalls and other animals made small movement noises obscuring any sounds Marian might make.

I tried using other senses to find my quarry. I took a deep breath, hoping to capture a hint of the perfume he carried about him. Nothing, but I'd hardly expected it in the barn. The scent of the animals came too strongly. I saw nothing, but touching a rough support beam convinced me that Marian moved overhead, in the loft. The faint vibrations didn't give any indication where in the loft he was, however. I'd have to do better to locate him exactly.

"Why'd you do it, Marian?" I called out. I wasn't going to insult his intelligence by offering a deal. He and I both knew what was in store for him. Traitors in AXE are eliminated. We are too highly trained for anything else. No prison in the world could hold one of our agents for long, and Hawk could never allow the information stored in any one agent's head to be turned over to the highest bidder.

"Why else, Carter? Money. Lots of it. Colonel Rokarov is very generous. And you know my hobbies. Women are expensive creatures. I find that the older I get, the more they expect me to have money and the willingness to spend it lavishly on them."

"He set up your coup in Southeast Asia, didn't he? He sacrificed his own agents and freed ours to put you into position to aid him."

"Of course, Carter. That's part of the price for my working with the Soviets. I needed a good cover to keep everyone from being suspicious when I failed to find the Australian radar station."

"You must have done more than that to arouse Hawk's curiosity. He sent me in."

"That surprised me," Marian admitted.

I heard small movement in the loft above. I thought it might have been a mouse until a tiny drop of blood spatted into the hay not ten feet in front of me. The wounded man moved into position for the kill.

"You got overconfident, Marian. Everything you did after I arrived was wrong. You had to give me too much information or I'd become suspicious of you right away."

"Not everything went wrong. I should have eliminated you and that meddling professor over the Nullarbor. I miscalculated on that."

"The time-delay went wrong, all right. Sending me out to Marston's station was your biggest mistake. I identified Claire's perfume as the same you reeked with in Sydney. You had been out here many times."

"She's quite a good lover for all her naîveté," said Marian. "I'd arranged with her father for the radar station. Things simply progressed from there."

"You used her as a hold on Marston."

"But of course."

I fired four times directly overhead. The heavy slugs ripped through boards and whined on up into the barn's roof. I heard Marian's scurrying footsteps as he changed position again. His ploy to get directly over me and shoot down hadn't worked.

As if nothing had happened, I continued talking. I still needed a positive location on the man before I tried for the kill.

"Other things made me certain. The radio dial was set on our contact frequency. I didn't know if Claire or Marston—or the Russians—had been calling you. But what really convinced me was the way Rokarov simply gave up after I captured him. He was waiting for reinforcements, all right. You."

I moved to the base of the ladder leading to the loft. Going up now might be hazardous to my health. I pictured Marian lying in wait, ready to put a single bullet through my head the instant I appeared at the top. In spite of this grim mental image, I started up, making sure that the creaking ladder creaked to the utmost.

"All circumstantial evidence, Carter. You'll never make any of it stick."

"You mean you're going to kill me and take the credit for destroying the radar station."

"I suppose I must kill Rokarov, too. A pity. He's a very influential man in the KGB."

Rather than going on over the top and getting a few bullets pumped into me, I stuck Wilhelmina into my belt and moved hand over hand along the edge of the loft until I was ten feet away from the ladder. With a large kick and a convulsive jerk of my shoulders, I hurled over the edge and landed in the loft.

The move took Marian by surprise. I had time to pull out my pistol, raise the muzzle and fire. Every movement felt as if I'd been dipped in molasses, but Marian's movements were similarly slow. Every detail etched permanently on my mind. I saw the bullet hole I'd put in his shoulder, the shallow groove on the side of his head from my second shot, the way his lips pulled back in a feral snarl, the slight quiver in his hand, the tiny pearl-handled automatic. I saw it all.

My Luger bucked hard against my hand and shattered the slow motion movements.

Sanford Marian jerked erect, arms outstretched. He dropped his gun and staggered back. This was enough to send him out the open hayloft door. He hung suspended in midair until gravity seized his lifeless body and pulled it down.

"You stupid son of a bitch," I said, looking down at his broken form on the ground. I slipped the safety back on Wilhelmina and started back down the ladder, heading for the house.

THIRTY-TWO

"She's resting," said Daniela, sitting beside me on the sofa in the front room of the Marston house. "She's been through a lot today, and she's not taking it well."

Claire Marston was an innocent victim of all that had happened. Her mother's death had started a chain reaction as certain—and as deadly—as any atomic reaction. Ram Marston had spent most of his money trying to keep his wife alive. When she'd died, the station had been in serious financial straits. But it provided the only link the man had to his past, his memories, his wife.

Claire had felt trapped out here. When Marston and Sanford Marian entered their illicit deal, Claire had been overjoyed at the occasional visits by the AXE agent. I had to hand it to Marian. He had a way with women. Suave, cool, debonair, he was everything Claire had come to expect in the European men she'd met while in school. He'd swept her off her feet.

And used her as an added lever against her father.

"Your world is violent, Nick," said Daniela in a low voice. "I'm not sure I'd enjoy it."

Again the woman surprised me.

"Enjoy it? What do you mean?"

"We hit it off pretty well."

"You can say that," I agreed.

"And I thought, after this assignment of yours, maybe we could team up."

"Working on my future assignments?"

"Something like that. But I don't think I'm cut out for it. I understand now—a little—what went on here. I'm glad there are men like you who can defend us."

I hesitated mentioning Elaine Thompson over in New Zealand. The idea that a woman with my cold-blooded instincts existed might be too much for Daniela. She fancied herself a woman of the world, able to roll with the punches, to do anything at all any man can do. Or she had until she met me. She had to qualify "anything at all" to "almost anything." She wanted desperately to believe no woman could perform my job simply because she, Dr. Daniela Rhys-Smith, couldn't,

Elaine Thompson would come as a real jolt to her.

"So you've decided to stay at your university post?"

"No, I don't think so. That's a dead end for me. I want to work with the aborigines. I . . . I feel akin to them. I understand and appreciate them. They're a violent, uncivilized lot, but I empathize with them."

"You're saying you feel better among violent, uncivilized men than among civilized, violent ones like me?"

She paused, then nodded.

"In a way," I told her, "you've climbed onto a treadmill. You've found out about the radar station and Vladen Rokarov and Sanford Marian and Marston. And about me."

"You're going to have to kill me, too?" Her voice sounded small and frightened, like a tiny animal trapped and awaiting its hunter.

"Nothing like that. But I do have to swear you to secrecy. You can't go blabbing this around."

She relaxed visibly.

"I can handle that. I'm not sure I'd *want* to talk about this, Nick. I'm afraid it'll give me nightmares, as is."

"It gives me constant nightmares," I said softly. And it did. This job isn't for the squeamish, especially when it comes to treachery from people you've counted on as being your allies.

The radio, which I'd moved into the house, let out a squeal of electronic rage.

"Excuse me, Daniela. I'm being summoned. Back in a minute."

I went into the bedroom that had once been Ram Marston's and sat in front of the transmitter. I picked up the microphone and said, "N3 speaking, over."

"Report, N3. I've received the preliminary. I need a concise one to pass along to the President." David Hawk sounded as if he'd asked me to pick up a loaf of bread from the grocery from him.

"It turned a bit wet, sir," I started. "I'm afraid· the aborigine population has been reduced significantly since I arrived."

"That is being taken care of. Continue."

"The four remaining Soviet technicians and Colonel Rokarov are being kept in one of their own storerooms. I check on them periodically. I'm awaiting the arrival of the AXE team to take over."

"ETA, four hours, N3. Continue."

"Well, sir, I had the idea that, rather than dismantle the station, we might continue to use it."

"Go on, N3."

"The Australians are chary about giving out their test data from Woomera, and they do have some sophisticated listening posts of their own over at Carnarvon."

"Yes, they were the first to pick up Armstrong's message from the moon, weren't they?" mused Hawk, as if I told him something he hadn't already known.

"This radar unit might prove useful in the future. And, after all, it *is* already established."

"That requires the cooperation of the owner of the sheep station. Marston is dead, is he not?"

"I eliminated him, yes, sir. But the station isn't going to stay in the family. I'm sure Claire Marston will want to sell it. She's not cut out to live on the frontier."

"I see. You're suggesting that AXE buy the station from her, then sell it to a front?"

"Essentially correct, sir."

"And who might this front be, N3?"

"Daniela Rhys-Smith. She wants to continue her researches into the aborigines. It's a perfect cover."

"I'm sure," Hawk said dryly. "I'll consider this proposal."

"Sir?" I asked, hesitating to even mention the next item.

"Go on. The drift is catching up with us. Either speak up or I'll have to arrange for a different comsat to relay."

"How much did you know about Sanford Marian? Before I came?"

"Not enough, Nick." When he used my name, I knew he was talking off the record. "I had some suspicions, nothing more. It's not good to accuse a field agent with his background of turning traitor without more than tenuous supposition, yet a top agent turning traitor won't give more than that to go on. I sent you in to find out for certain, one way or the other. The radar station was of secondary importance, as you probably realize now."

"It turned out well, sir."

"Eminently so. Capturing the station, Rokarov, and eliminating Marian reaffirms my faith in you, Nick."

"But you still had Elaine Thompson over in New Zealand as backup, in case Marian did me in?"

"N3, I run a tight operation. I go by the book. As to how you found out about Thompson, I won't ask. But in the future, please refrain from parading such information out before me. I might *have* to ask. However you got it, that couldn't have affected your dealings with Marian."

"Yes, it did. Simple deduction. Three AXE agents for one mission was two too many. That meant I had to be sent in to find out if Marian had gone bad. If he got me, then Elaine got him."

"As you said, N3, simple." Hawk paused, then added, "One last thing. When the team arrives, see that Rokarov is sent off immediately. I have a submarine meeting him just off the Great Barrier Reef."

"It'll be done, sir."

"Be back in Washington in three days, N3. I have another mission for you."

"Uh, sir, that might not be possible."

"What?"

"It seems that a delay might be better to keep from arousing suspicion about the station."

"You're saying your presence is required for a longer duration? How much longer, N3?"

"A week should do it, sir."

Hawk sighed and said, "Very well. Out."

I smiled and turned off the radio.

"It's been great this week, Nick," said Daniela. "So much has happened, I can hardly believe it."

The AXE team had removed the Russian technicians and Rokarov. For the time being, the radar unit was unattended. I'd told them I'd act as watchman. In the meantime, Claire Marston sold the station to an elderly—and fictitious—person in Adelaide, who conveniently "died," leaving the station to Daniela Rhys-Smith, so that she might pursue her investigations into aborigine culture.

"I'm rich, Nick, and more. This week with you has been super. Do you think you'll be back. Soon?" Her brown eyes glistened with tears.

I kissed her. It had been a great week, just us—and Pierce's mob—on the station.

"I'll be back to see how you're doing. But soon? That I don't know."

I kissed her again, solemnly shook hands with Pierce, then hurried to climb into the single engine plane. If I stayed another ten seconds, I might want to stay for another week.

I revved the engine, taxied and became airborne. The last sight of the Australian Outback I remember is Daniela surrounded by Pierce's tribe, waving goodbye.

DON'T MISS THE NEXT NEW
NICK CARTER SPY THRILLER

HIDE AND GO DIE

There are limits to the amount of manipulation the human psyche can tolerate. I had swallowed all the humility I could stomach. That Theo had controlled the battle so far was enough to handle. That my own instincts had betrayed me was more than I could endure.

It was just not possible that Theo would let that material get into enemy hands! It was insanity to its most ludicrous extreme. I shot a glance toward the defector, feeling capable at that moment of tearing him to pieces.

But the look on Theo's face brought me up short. He was obviously no more comfortable with what he was seeing than I was. For the first time, there was a visible crack in his omnipotent shell. Another quick look, this time to Leslie, confirmed the suspicion.

Kiang was there without invitation.

"What the hell are you . . . ?" Theo began, and then his face turned chalk white.

I whirled in the Oriental's direction, and my guts did a half-gainer.

We were all staring up the perforated barrel of a Czech ZK-466 machine gun.

"My apologies for this unexpected intrusion." He smiled with a slight bow.

"Don't be a fool, Kiang," Theo hissed.

The benign grin crumbled from the Oriental's face. "It is you, I'm afraid, who have been foolish. You mock us with your talk of honor—and then deal with the dog who comes to kill you! The dog and his bitch!"

The gun swiveled uncomfortably in my direction.

"Hold it, Kiang," I growled. "I'm a prisoner here. There are no deals. The bids are in, and I'm as ignorant as you of the outcome."

There was a tightening of his grip around the gun. "You lie!"

I looked quickly to Theo. "What the hell's going on?"

His only response was to lift his hand to silence me. The Oriental appeared to glean some kind of understanding in the gesture, because his tenseness seemed to drain. The barrel drooped only a few inches, but it was enough to give me a sense of reprieve.

"Perhaps you speak the truth," he said uncertainly. "But this is still a room of lies."

"Why are you so certain you've been deceived?" I hissed, feeling the anger rising inside me.

It was Theo to whom the answer was directed. "It is beyond the power of the Occidental to ever fathom the Oriental mind. Your guard could lead me through a hundred mazes, and I would still clear my mind and remember. So I followed him, speaking with my mouth but learning with my senses. And when your man came to claim my bid, I let him go. But I silenced the guard, took his weapon, and returned to watch . . . to test the sincerity of your so-called honor." And then a laugh filled with contempt burst from him. "Honor! The bids flew home, like five tiny sparrows, but when your man again went out, it was not to me. You have left me with no choice. What you will not give me in honor, I will take with force!"

The gun turned in my direction and leveled itself at my chest. I don't really know what it was I expected out of that moment. Irony, I guess.

But what I got instead was Theo's firm and chilling

voice, the same voice that had turned Julio Martinez' blood to ice, the voice that steals your will.

"If you are going to pull that trigger, now would be as good a time as any."

The room exploded with a single blast. For me time dropped to a crawl, a slow-motion hell. In spite of every instinct to the contrary, my eyes did not shut, my body did not retreat. Instead, I watched my expected death like a casual spectator. My eyes traced the bullet from the gun, watching it as it left the barrel and spiraled toward my chest. Such is the brief mirage of one's own demise.

—From HIDE AND GO DIE
A New Nick Carter Spy Thriller
From Charter in April

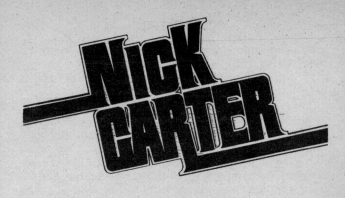

☐ 01948-X	**THE AMAZON**	$2.50	
☐ 05381-5	**BEIRUT INCIDENT**	$2.25	
☐ 10505-X	**THE CHRISTMAS KILL**	$2.50	
☐ 13935-3	**DAY OF THE DINGO**	$1.95	
☐ 14172-2	**THE DEATH STAR AFFAIR**	$2.50	
☐ 14169-2	**DEATHLIGHT**	$2.50	
☐ 15676-2	**DOCTOR DNA**	$2.50	
☐ 15244-9	**THE DOMINICAN AFFAIR**	$2.50	
☐ 17014-5	**THE DUBROVNIK MASSACRE**	$2.25	
☐ 18124-4	**EARTH SHAKER**	$2.50	

A8